What people are saying about *Becoming Bob:*

In this satisfying conclusion to the *Allister of Turtle Mountain* series, we see how persistence, patience, and faith lead to the fulfillment of a young man's dreams. I recommend this book for middle schoolers, who will be captivated by the action-filled life of the pioneer farmers. They'll identify with Allister's struggle to chart a different future than the one his parents intend for him. As they're drawn into the story, the students will absorb historical knowledge the easy way—by living it vicariously.

—Connie Lee
Educator, freelance writer
2008 winner of the Guideposts Writers Workshop contest

Readers who have grown attached to Allister in the first two books in the *Allister of Turtle Mountain* series will enjoy watching him mature as he pursues his dream of an education while continuing to long for his father's support. Engagingly written, the story of Allister's busy life in the city, changing relationships with family members, and growing faith in God make for a fine finish to the series.

—Jill Schramm
Newspaper journalist for forty years
and senior staff writer for *Minot Daily News* in Minot, ND

I0628564

Allister of Turtle Mountain Series - Book 3

Becoming Bob

Patricia E. Linson

BECOMING BOB
Copyright © 2019 by Patricia E. Linson

Print ISBN: 978-1-4866-1638-1

Word Alive Press
119 De Baets Street, Winnipeg, MB R2J 3R9
www.wordalivepress.ca

WORD ALIVE
—PRESS—

Cataloguing in Publication may be obtained through Library and Archives Canada

Dedication

In loving memory
of
Robert A. McRuer

His favourite scripture was:

*"But seek ye first the kingdom of God, and his righteousness;
and all these things shall be added unto you."*
—Matthew 6:33

He was a man who demonstrated the following truth with his life:

*"He that is slow to anger is better than the mighty;
and he that ruleth his spirit than he that taketh a city."*
—Proverbs 16:32

Contents

Book III: August, 1895–September, 1902

Acknowledgements

With gratitude, I remember my grandfather, Robert A. McRuer, who shared with me many anecdotal scenes from his life as a teen in southwestern Manitoba.

His daughter, Reta McRuer (deceased), gave me a copy of a biographical sketch of her father that she had written for the Manitoba Historical Society in 1990. She also wrote additional notes about him for me in 2008 and provided several McRuer family photos.

I wish to thank Henry Titcombe, my father, for giving me his written version of the anecdotes Robert A. McRuer had told him.

With gratitude, I remember my mother, Jean Titcombe (deceased), for giving me access to a formal portrait of her father, Robert A. McRuer. She also confirmed that her Uncle John was often called Angus.

Irene Patterson (deceased), niece of Robert A. McRuer, and Gordon McRuer (deceased), nephew of Robert A. McRuer, provided photos of the McRuer farmhouse with its brick veneer and the earlier log barn and later large barn with its plank sides and stone foundation. In addition, Gordon McRuer gave me *Beckoning Hills: Pioneer Settlement Turtle Mountain Souris-Basin Areas* and its attached maps.

I wish to thank Michelle Scott, head librarian at Boissevain and Morton Regional Library. She located articles about the McRuer family and put me in touch with Gordon McRuer. She also gave me copies of archival photos of the schools Robert A. McRuer attended.

I remember with gratitude Bob McRuer (deceased), my uncle and Robert A. McRuer's son, for loaning me his father's cash journal. My thanks to Grace Van Dyck, Bob McRuer's daughter, for helping her father locate that journal and for sending it to me.

I thank Dr. Gordon Goldsborough of the Manitoba Historical Society for information regarding brick makers in southwestern Manitoba in the 1890s.

I am grateful to Dr. Bruce Brandsness, dentist, for information on historically-appropriate dental pain controllers.

I wish to thank the 2008 summer staff of the John E. Robbins Library at the University of Brandon, Brandon, Manitoba, for keeping the library open long enough for me to access information about Manitoba's 1890 school curriculum.

I am grateful for my husband, Irv, who helped with proofreading the manuscript of *Becoming Bob*.

I thank my friend and former neighbour, Donna Larson, for cleaning my house while I worked on the original draft of this book. I also thank Miriam and Abraham for cleaning my house while I rewrote sections of the text.

I thank the members of the writers' critique group in Shoreview, Minnesota, for their suggestions for this book. I owe a special debt of gratitude to Karen Schulz, Wes Erwin, and Sue Shetka for their extra work on the latter half of the text.

My thanks to Patricia Schwartz, my art class instructor, for her assistance with the creation of the cover illustration for *Becoming Bob*.

I appreciate Sylvia St.Cyr of Word Alive Press, and Kerry Wilson, editor, for their assistance in the publication of *Becoming Bob*.

chapter one

Rebuffed

Manitoba, August, 1895

"Father, Mother, could I talk to you a moment?" Allister straddled a bench next to the kitchen table, opposite from where his father sat sipping a cup of tea and reading.

Without lifting his head, Father grumped. "Allister, you've got chores to do."

"Um ... this won't take long."

"Alright!" Father put down his newspaper and frowned at Allister. "What is it?"

Mother stopped clearing the supper dishes and sat beside Father.

Allister cleared his throat, then blurted, "I want more schooling."

His parents looked at each other, their surprise registering.

His father's frown became a scowl. "You graduated eighth grade at the end of June!"

"True ... but I'd like to go to high school too. Next month."

"High school? Nobody in our family has ever gone to high school. Besides, what farmer needs high school?" Mr. McRuer returned to his paper.

Allister gulped. *He assumes that NO farmer needs more than a Grade 8 education!*

Mother turned towards her husband and put her hand on his arm. "Allister is a bright lad, Father. He did well in school. Has his nose in a book every chance he gets. High school might be just what this son needs."

"The closest high school is in Cherry Creek, twelve miles away," Father growled at Mother, then glared at Allister over the top edge of the newspaper.

"Please, Father. I would really like to go."

"Where would you stay? We've no relatives in that town." Father flung his paper down, sending his tea cup flying. Looking at Mother again, he added, "You do agree that at fourteen he's too young to leave home, don't you?"

Mother didn't answer.

"Mother?" Allister felt his desperation rising. *Why doesn't she say something? I thought she would support me.*

She merely shrugged. Without looking at either Father or Allister, she reached for the cup and saucer.

Allister sat with shoulders slumped and his mouth hanging open. *No, no, no!*

Not about to give up, Allister stammered, "Father, I-I'm sure I c-can ..."

Slamming both hands on the table and leaning towards Allister, Father interrupted him with raised voice. "Who of all seven of my children do I have left to help me run this farm? Mary's married. Will's gone. Dan's about to leave. John's started his own homestead claim. You and Jim are all that's left."

And little Jessie, Allister thought, but didn't dare say. "But, F-father, I-I w-want ..."

Turning red in the face, Father pounded on the table and hollered, "No, you are NOT going anywhere! Stop arguing. Do your chores!"

Allister felt disappointment flooding his soul and drowning the light out of his eyes and face.

Heading for the back door, he glanced over his shoulder before he opened it. Father sat rooted in the same spot. To Allister's astonishment, he saw his mother reach across the table to touch his father's hand. Blinking back tears and swallowing hard, Allister left to finish his chores, muttering, "I had hoped she would stand up to Father, support my efforts for a better future."

Later, after everyone else was back in the house, Allister took a lit lantern from the barn and set it on a sawhorse next to the remaining stack of cordwood behind the house. Taking his frustration out on the kindling, he split wood into the night. John came out once to stop him.

"Leave me alone!" Allister shouted, sure John could see his face still wet from the anger and tears he couldn't control.

"Just be careful," John reminded him gently. "A severed toe or foot won't help you deal with whatever made you angry."

Last to bed and the first up at dawn, Allister did his share of the chores, took some leftover biscuits and scones to nibble on the way, and walked the mile cross-country to Dan's homestead. By helping his older brother, Allister figured he could get some time and space to calm down. Even then, he wasn't sure how to deal with his loss of hope. He leaned against the shovel in his hand, looked out over the wide-open prairie, and thought it ironic that the very panorama he'd admired the previous evening now felt like a smothering force. *The demands of the land have squashed my dreams. Will anyone besides mother ever understand why I feel this way?*

When Dan arrived later, he tried to get Allister to tell him what had happened the night before.

With an exasperated look, Allister muttered through tight lips, "Let me work with you without asking me any questions, alright?"

Keeping conversation to the minimum, Allister worked alongside Dan on the frame for his farmhouse.

At noon, Dan offered to share with Allister what Mother had packed. "She would've packed more if she'd known you'd come here," Dan said.

"When you go back home tonight, please tell Mother and Father that I'm helping you for a few days. Ask her to pack some extra for me for dinner tomorrow."

"Aren't you going home for supper?"

"No. I'm going to visit Mary and Joe."

The afternoon of framing passed quickly enough. As he worked, Allister felt his body relax. But he wasn't sure if either he or his father could face each other calmly just yet.

Late afternoon, Allister ambled over to his sister's homestead. During his walk, Allister mentally reviewed the series of events of the previous day. *Was there anything I could have done differently?*

chapter two

Allister's Epiphany

Yesterday morning, I remember feeling a small sense of achievement. I had finally figured out the rhythm of the dump rake I was driving. Release the rake's metal pedal. Wait while its tines gather a mound of stalks, and at the right moment, push the pedal forward to raise the tines so the stalks fall clear. Then release the pedal again. My windrows are now straight, making it easier to fork the dried grass onto a hay rack later.

Even becoming successful at one more farming task wasn't enough. I was beginning to believe only more schooling would satisfy me. Yes, I was happy when I graduated from Grade 8 at Wood Lake School. That event was only two months ago, but it feels more like a decade has passed.

On our Dominion Day holiday in July, when my older brother Dan caught me staring through a classroom window in the Cherry Creek High School, he advised me to forget about school. He said to give myself time to settle into our life on the farm. Yet when I am honest with myself, I do not want to be a farmer.

For some reason, I am afraid to say so out loud. Farming is all I know. Would I be able to do anything else? Be a teacher? Or maybe even a preacher?

I shudder every time I think about our first day in Cherry Creek. We had just arrived from Lachute, Quebec. Jim and I had to act quickly to save the seriously injured driver, Peter McKinnon.

The driver's accident hasn't been the only life-threatening situation during the last three years. How well I remember the weeks Jim and I worked with my sister, Mary, to care for her very sick fiancé, Joe. Then in the middle of one night last spring, Father, Jim, and I helped one of our cows deliver a breech birth calf. When I asked Father how he knew to turn the calf, I was surprised to learn of the difficult birth of my little sister, Jessie. Manitoba definitely needs more doctors. Maybe I could become a doctor.

A teacher? A preacher? A doctor? Any one of those occupations will require more education, starting with high school. While I drove the dump rake, I remember saying out loud, "That's what I'll do. I'll go back to school." I also remember wondering if my parents would allow me to leave home next month.

A loud clanging interrupted my daydreaming. "It's noon and time for dinner, my friends," I said to the bays. After I unhitched Jake and Maggie from the dump rake and returned with the team to the barn, I thought I would talk with my parents about my idea after the meal.

Unfortunately, when I entered the house, I saw John, not Mother, tending the cook stove in the kitchen. I asked him where she was. He told me she'd taken Jessie and Tawny, the toonie puppy, to visit Mary. Said they'd be back by supper.

I remember thinking it was better to wait until Mother returned before I talked about more schooling. I'd need her support. So after we finished dinner, I went straight back to my raking job.

Just as I finished the field, the sun touched the horizon. Before turning towards the barnyard, I remember stopping the horses for a few moments to enjoy the sunset. Crimson, glowing-orange, gold, and pale-yellow danced after each other across the sky. Cricket and meadowlark songs filled the cooling air. A breeze lifted across the prairie and scented every corner of the field with the fragrance of fresh hay. Enjoying the moment with the prairie, I remember whispering, "Thank you, God, for this beauty. Please help my parents let me leave the farm to go to high school."

After supper, I delayed leaving the kitchen so I could talk to my parents.

How was I to know that asking them for permission to continue my education would ignite such a firestorm of refusal from Father?

I had waited for Mother's return because I thought she would be the one person in the family who'd support me. Yet she had hardly said a word. What more could I have done?

How will the other members of my family react?

chapter three

Gathering Guidance

While Allister waited at Mary and Joe's door for an answer to his knock, he wondered, *What will Mary say? Will she offer her support?*

Although Mary's face registered her surprise to see him, Allister felt welcome and gladly accepted her invitation to join her and Joe for supper. During the meal, Allister admitted one of the things he'd missed the last two years was her cooking. Mary and Joe just laughed at the compliment.

"Well," Joe said, "don't you think her cooking looks really good on me?"

"How much weight have you gained?" Allister asked, eyeing his brother-in-law.

"Oh, at least thirty," the farmer said, grinning. He invited Allister to keep him company while he did chores.

"In a bit," Allister said. "Need to talk to Mary for a while first."

"Alright," Joe said. "Come when you're ready."

After Joe left the house, Mary got up. "We can talk while we do the washing up, eh?"

"Sure, Mary."

As they worked together, she asked, "How are things going, Allister?"

"Really well. Dan has a good start on his homestead. Come October, he'll be ready to move in. John's started work on his own claim, but since it's right next to Father's, he doesn't need to be in a hurry to move out. Father's crops and cattle look great. Should bring in good prices this year. Mother's garden is doing well too. Jessie's got a little friend now, as you know."

Mary laughed. "Yes, I do. A toonie puppy she calls Tawny. Met the wiggly charmer yesterday. Should be good company for our little sister."

Mary paused, her hands resting on the edges of the wash basin, and turned towards Allister. "But what about you? How are you doing? You don't look so happy."

"I'm not."

"Why? You've graduated! Everybody's real proud of you!"

"I decided yesterday that Grade 8 shouldn't be the end of my education. I asked Father and Mother for permission to leave home and live in Cherry Creek so I could go to high school. Father got very angry. He shouted at me and even banged the table. Father's answer was a flat no! He also said that at fourteen, I am too young to move into town by myself."

Mary resumed the washing of the dishes. "You're not going to like what I have to say, but I agree with Father, Allister. You *are* too young to leave home just yet. Wait a little and ask again. You're a smart boy. If more schooling is what you really want, don't give up."

She knows me well! Would I ever want to hear such advice? Allister fumed. *No way!* Even though dismayed by his older sister's words, he understood she was giving him her usual level-headed take on his situation.

When they had finished the washing up, Allister thanked Mary for her advice and went out to the barn to help Joe with chores. "Is it alright for me to spend the night?" he asked.

"Do your parents know where you are?"

"Dan and I worked together today on his house. Before he left to go home for supper, I told him to tell my parents I was visiting you and Mary."

"Then it's alright with me."

At the end of the next day, Allister walked home with Dan—a mile cross-country along the edges of the rolling fields of his brother's neighbours. After two days to think about everything and having had a talk with Mary, Allister had formed a general plan. *I'll wait. Maybe one of the Wood Lake School's teachers can help me study the ninth grade while I'm waiting.*

Allister's parents said nothing about his disappearance. He figured his mother, at least, understood why he'd walked off. He saw John look quizzically at him now and again, but his older brother didn't ask any questions. Jessie seemed the most aware of Allister's gloomy mood. Her reaction was to hug him spontaneously from time to time. She invited him to play with her and Tawny or take walks with them.

Allister's twin, Jim, turned out to be the least sympathetic. When Allister told him about the argument with their parents, Jim shrugged. "I said you probably couldn't do it. Why are you so upset? There's nothing wrong with this life. Enjoy it!"

With the beginning of harvest merely days away, John asked Allister to accompany him by riding bareback on one of the harnessed team to Cherry Creek to pick up his new wagon and bring it to the farm. When they entered the town that Saturday, Allister begged for some time to run an errand of his own while John tended to other business.

It'd been not quite two years since Allister had last returned a borrowed book to Reverend Wood, the vicar of St. Matthew's Anglican Church, one of the largest buildings facing the main street of the town. Made of stone, the church's bell tower and tall, stained-glass windows gave it an imposing appearance. As Allister creaked a wooden door open and walked among multi-coloured dapples of light down one aisle of the silent sanctuary, he wondered if his old friend would still be there.

Standing at the door of Reverend Wood's study, Allister took a deep breath and knocked. A chair scraped against the floor, and the door opened. "Young Robert," the Reverend said, smiling and reaching for Allister's hand. "How are you? Do come in!"

The vicar's remembering to call him Robert warmed Allister's heart. *During my first visit to his office three years ago, I told Reverend Wood*

my real first name is Robert, and it's the name I prefer to be called. He remembers.
Imagine that! I'm already glad I've come.

Once they were both seated, the vicar said, "Reverend Forsythe has stopped by from time to time and spoken of his church at Wood Lake School and your family. He made mention of a wedding—your sister, Mary's, I believe. It had a rather exciting beginning. He told me about a runaway buggy with the bride in it ... and the groom chasing after on his horse?"

"Oh yes!" Allister's gloomy mood vaporized as he revisited the scene. A chuckle bubbled up.

The vicar's recall of Mary's mishap served as the pulling of a cork. Starting with the story of the wily horse's, Shalazar's, escapade, Allister related incident after incident from the previous two years. He'd forgotten how easy it was to talk to Reverend Wood and how much he'd missed their conversations. Allister even told the vicar about the decision he'd made in the hay field and the argument he'd had with his parents afterward.

"Have you ever told your father plainly that you don't want to be a farmer?"

"No. I'm afraid it'd make him angry, maybe hurt his feelings."

"A wise lad."

"I've tried to tell my twin brother, Jim, but he doesn't understand or support me at all!"

Lacing fingers together at his waist, Reverend Wood appeared thoughtful. Allister waited, noticing that his elderly friend still wore a collarless shirt with rolled up sleeves, suspenders, ordinary pants, and moccasins for his Saturday sermon preparation, just like he had when Allister first came to visit a little over three years ago.

"Maybe that's because you two are so close," the vicar added. "You've done almost everything together—up 'til now. He can't imagine you doing something completely separate from him in the future."

"But why can't he see it?" Allister frowned. "We've both known our whole lives that we're very different on the inside. I love to read and learn; he doesn't. He loves horses, any horse; I don't like or trust most of them. Farming is enough of a mental challenge for him. It isn't for me. I'm already bored with it!

"I visited my sister, Mary, and told her about asking for permission to leave to go to high school. She agreed with our father about me being too young to leave home. But she also said to not give up. Her advice was to wait until I'm older."

The vicar smiled, nodded, and leaned back in his chair. "Sounds like you've already gotten some good advice, Robert.

"Some time ago, you mentioned that Randy, a neighbour of Will's, gave you a Bible. Have you read any of it?"

"Yes, Genesis and Exodus. Got stuck," Allister admitted, wrinkling his nose. "Skipped to other books in the Old Testament. Read some of the stories my mother taught in Sunday school."

"That's good," Reverend Wood commented. "And I agree with you. It's difficult to read straight through the Bible." The vicar chuckled. "Leviticus isn't the most exciting read."

Looking at Allister over the tops the rimless spectacles he now wore, the vicar asked, "Have you tried reading the New Testament? Start with the Gospel of Mark. When you come across a sentence that means a lot to you, underline it like this." He picked up the well-thumbed Bible that lay open on his desk and handed it to Allister.

He couldn't believe all the markings he saw. "You've even written notes in the margins!" Allister said as he handed it back.

"In school, the teachers warn students against writing in any book. That's because the next student to use that book would be distracted by all the markings. But you can and should mark any book that's yours, especially ones you have no plans to pass on or sell."

"Sir, the last time I visited you, you said I could borrow another book. Is that offer still open?"

The vicar nodded and scanned the spines of a stack of books on the floor. "Here's a good one."

"Another by Charles Dickens. *Great Expectations*."

Reverend Wood nodded and smiled. "Robert, in the first chapter you will meet a boy named Pip. In the opening scene, Pip is visiting tombstones in a churchyard. Why do you suppose a boy would go there?"

"To visit the grave of a family member?"

"Yes … in fact, those of almost his whole family. Yet Mr. Dickens entitled his book *Great Expectations*. How could young Pip have any hope for his future without a supporting family?"

Allister clasped the book. "Guess I'll read and find out. Thank you for the book—and for listening, too. Better run. John will be wondering what's keeping me."

While Allister rode with his oldest brother in the new wagon towards home, John asked, "What's going on with you? Wood chopping late at night? Running off to Dan's, then Mary's?"

Gulping down his reluctance to share his feelings with this brother, Allister answered truthfully. "I'm frustrated with my life, and I'm angry at Father. I told him I want to go to high school. He gave me a flat no! Said I couldn't go."

"Did he say why?"

"He said a farmer doesn't need more education. He said he couldn't afford to lose any more hands. He also said that at fourteen, I'm too young to leave home."

"I don't know if he's right about the first reason, but he's right about the second and the third. Why do you want high school?"

"Don't want to farm. It's not only hard work, it's also very boring. I need a mental challenge."

John grinned. "And you are sure you won't get that on the farm? What about all the calculating we've had to do to construct all the fences and buildings on our claims? The estimations of costs in seed and feed against the potential profits on the sale of our grain and livestock? Those aren't enough of a mental challenge for you?"

Allister frowned and didn't say anything.

"What about the smarts it takes to figure out the best way to train a particular horse?" John added.

For a few moments, Allister stared across the panorama of alternating patches of waving prairie grass and grain that rose towards the distant Turtle Mountain. Then he turned to face his older brother, exasperation adding an edge to his voice. "Honestly, John, you're describing Jim. Not me. I want something more."

Spelling out some of his wishes to John gave Allister a profound sense of relief. Even if this brother didn't understand him, Allister had expressed clearly for the first time how he really felt to a family member.

John sat silently the rest of the way home. Allister knew from past experience the silence meant his older brother was mentally measuring all the angles of the problem. *John did figure out ways to support Will and Dan yet remain loyal to Father.* Allister wondered, *Could John ever become supportive of me in my reach for my own goals?*

chapter four

An Itinerant Pitcher

"**C**ome on, Jim." Allister handed his brother a bucket. "Threshing crew is here. Gotta fill the water tank for the steam engine."

While he and Jim filled, carried, and dumped bucket after bucket from the windmill pump into the huge metal tank, Allister thought about his first year as a full-time farmer. *Because last year's crop was so plentiful, Father and John had to build extra grain bins. A month ago, we hauled the remaining sacks of last year's wheat to the elevators in Desford and Cherry Creek. All the bins are empty and ready in time for this year's harvest. From the looks of our fields, we'll need every inch of space in those bins. Farming full-time seems to have been good for both Jim and me, although I'd hate to admit it out loud. We're taller. Stronger. At least Jim is. I'm guessing I am, too. No machine, horse, or Angus is a problem for me anymore. And whether I want it or not, I am being forced to grow something else every farmer must have plenty of—patience.*

With two brimming buckets in hand, Allister stepped towards the tank but halted when he felt a momentary pressure on his leg. He looked down in time to see Jessie's little Sheltie herd her mistress away from Allister, his buckets, and the water tank's wheels. "Oh hi, Tawny," Allister said. "What a good girl!"

"Jessie," Jim said, "please stay away from the machines. Tell you what. Go find Caroline. She's come to give Mother a hand in the kitchen. Maybe you can help too. There will be lots of men to feed today."

"Alright, Jim." Jessie walked as quickly as she could towards the house, with Tawny following close behind.

Allister waited until he was sure his little sister was far enough away to not hear what he wanted to say. "Good thing Jessie has Tawny. That dog has developed amazing techniques for keeping our sister out of trouble."

When the tank was full, Allister and Jim hitched up Jake and Maggie and drove it out to the steam engine. Unhitching and riding the team over to an empty wagon that sat among the rows of stooks in the field, Allister and Jim studied the strangers who had accompanied the threshing crew regulars.

"Father says our workers this year will include itinerant men from Ontario," Jim said.

"I know. I heard." Allister frowned. *Hope the ones here aren't like the stories I've heard about such men—drinkers and cussers. Mother won't put up with such behaviour. I don't like it much, either.*

This year, Allister and Jim worked some of the time with the pitchers on the hay wagon. Dealing with the golden cascade from the back of the thresher had both of them scrambling. Allister was glad that they were working with a couple of experienced men, one of whom said he was from Ontario.

When it was time for dinner break, the crew chief hollered at one of the other men who had been forking the straw. "Hey, reverend! How about saying the meal's blessing?"

The pitcher walked into the middle of the circle of men and boys, took off his hat, and bowed his head. While the man prayed, Allister opened one eye to peer at "the reverend," studying him from the top of his dark brown hair down his red and black plaid shirt and faded overalls to the tip of his dusty boots. Focusing on the man's very ordinary appearance, Allister missed every word the man said. *He doesn't look like anybody special.*

After running errands for his mother, Allister took his plate of dinner and sat next to the "reverend." Between bites, Allister asked, "Why do they call you reverend?"

"Kind of a strange nickname to stick on a guy who isn't one. Maybe it's because I like to talk to everyone about Jesus. My name's actually Sam Pollack."

"Mine's Allister McRuer."

"Glad to meet you, Allister. What do you plan to do with your life?"

Fifteen-year-old Allister gasped. *No one's ever asked me that before.* "Don't want to farm," he blurted. "Don't like the animals. I want to do something else, but don't know if I'll ever get to."

A blast from the steam engine interrupted their conversation.

"Well, Allister, we've got to get back to work. Talk to you some other time perhaps."

Allister nodded. "Perhaps."

———————

After supper that evening, Allister went with his father and brothers to do chores and take care of the extra teams. When he returned from the south pasture, Allister stopped by Sam's tent, since he was one of pitchers who camped on their farm that night.

"Hello, Mr. Pollack. Is now a good time to talk?"

Sam flipped up his tent door and pointed at a folded blanket on the grassy floor. "Certainly. Have a seat. But don't call me Mr. Pollack. Sam will do."

Allister smiled. "Alright, Sam."

"At dinner break, Allister, you mentioned that you don't really want to farm," Sam said. "What would you rather do?"

"Go to high school." Allister hesitated, then stammered, "Be-become a d-doctor, but I haven't told my family that."

For the next few minutes, he described the decision he had made out in the hay field the previous summer and the discussion he'd had with his parents about his future.

"From what I see you doing now," Sam said after a moment of silence, "you are honouring your parents by obeying them. God sees your obedience and, at some point, will reward you for it."

"At first, when my father said I couldn't leave home to go to high school, I was very angry and upset. Felt there was no hope for my life. I went to visit my older sister, Mary. She encouraged me to not give up on my dream, but to wait."

"Thank the Lord for the wise women He has put in our lives!"

"That's true. And God's given me more than one—my mother, too. Well, goodnight, sir."

"Call me Sam—not reverend, not sir."

"Alright, Sam."

"Goodnight, Allister."

Hmm, Allister thought, *this man, Sam, seems nothing like the stories I've heard about itinerant threshers from Ontario. Usually rough men. Cursers, drinkers, brawlers. But I haven't heard Sam curse or say a harsh word to anyone. He treats Mother, Caroline, and Mary courteously. He's the first to volunteer for the hardest jobs. And I saw no evidence of strong drink on him, not even in his tent.*

———————

At dinner the next day, Allister asked his new friend about one phrase that had stuck in his mind and wouldn't let go. "Sam, when we first met, you said you like to tell everyone about Jesus. I already know a lot about Him. I go to church and help Mother with Sunday school. I often ask God for help, just like Reverend Wood in Cherry Creek urged me to do. I'm reading the Bible that Randy, my brother Will's neighbour, gave me. For school programs, I've recited several Bible passages. I know about Jesus, but ... what do you tell people about Him?"

Reaching into the pocket of his long-sleeved shirt hanging from the hay wagon's end frame, Sam opened a thin, worn, leather-bound New Testament. "Better yet, I'll show you, if you'd like me to."

Allister nodded. "That would be great."

Sam patted the ground next to him. "Sit here, then, so we can both see."

After Allister had scooted over, Sam asked. "Read Romans yet?"

"Yes, but I didn't understand a lot of it."

"See if you can understand this verse." Sam pointed. "Please read it out loud."

"*For all have sinned, and come short of the glory of God,*"[1] Allister read.

"How many people are sinners?" Sam asked.

"All. Everybody." Allister frowned. *That means me too. But I thought sinners were people who were murderers or thieves.*

"When God says we all come short of His glory," Sam continued, "He doesn't spend any time comparing us with each other."

Allister shifted, suddenly uncomfortable. *Guess that's what I have been doing, thinking I am better than others.*

"Can any of us measure up to God and His standard of righteousness?" Sam asked. "No, because if we break even one of the Ten Commandments, we've broken the link (God's Law) between us and Him. We always come short of His measurements." Sam turned a few pages of the book. "Now let's take a look at this verse."

"*For the wages of sin is death,*" Allister read, "*but the gift of God is eternal life through Jesus Christ our Lord.*"[2]

"Allister, what is a wage?"

"Earnings. A worker earns money or some benefit."

"So the end result of sin and being a sinner is death, physical and spiritual death. That death results in permanent separation from God."

A feeling of doom settled over Allister. *All my life I have been earning death? It doesn't matter how good I try to be? What hope do I have? What hope does anyone have?*

"In the same verse, a gift is mentioned." Sam smiled at Allister. "Does the receiver have to earn a gift?"

"No, he can't. He doesn't need to; just puts out his hands and takes it."

Sam nodded. "That's absolutely right, Allister. And what is God's gift to us? What does the verse you just read say the gift is?"

Allister reread the verse and answered, "Eternal life."

"Who does that eternal life come through?"

"Jesus ... it says Jesus Christ our Lord." Allister's mouth dropped open. *I don't have to earn it. Eternal life is a gift. It's not hopeless, after all. How do I receive this gift? Go to church? Become a member of one? Pray? Read my*

21

Bible? Be baptized? Do good? That's what everyone has led me to believe, so far. But all of that is doing, trying to earn eternal life. Can't be the way.

"Now in another book, God talks about our part." Sam helped Allister find Ephesians and said, "Please read these two verses."

"For by grace are ye saved through faith; and that not of yourselves: it is the gift of God: not of works, lest any man should boast."[3]

Allister found it hard to believe what he was reading. *It can't be that simple.*

"Like you said before, God's gift of eternal life can't be earned," Sam continued. "God wants the credit. If a man could do it himself, he'd brag about it. He'd say, 'Look at me! Look at what I did!' No, our salvation, the forgiveness of our sins, is a gift, God's grace to us. How do we receive His gift?"

"It says by faith."

"What is faith?"

"Isn't it like trust? Believing that what someone says is really true?"

"I believe you're right. So then, the next question is: Can we, can you, place your faith in God, trust what He says is true? Let's see." Sam searched until he found a book towards the end of the New Testament. "This is from a letter that the apostle Paul wrote to his friend, Titus. He thought of this younger man as his son. Please read this one," Sam said, pointing.

"In hope of eternal life, which God, that cannot lie, promised before the world began,"[4] Allister read aloud.

Hmm. He reread the verse. *I think I have always believed God told the truth in the Bible. He certainly doesn't hide how ugly people can be towards each other. That truth is all through the stories I read in the Old Testament. But this verse also says God promised. What did He promise?*

"Since God created the world, had this plan in the making before time began, and is the author of eternal life and righteousness," Sam summarized, "you can trust Him. The verse says God is not able to lie. He always tells the truth, and He promised to give us hope for eternal life. What's more, God tells us how to have eternal life."

Allister smiled. *That is exactly what I would like to know.*

Sam flipped back towards the beginning of his New Testament. "Let's see what He says in the book called Acts. Please read this verse."

"*Neither is there salvation in any other: for there is none other name under heaven given among men, whereby we must be saved.*"⁵

"Who is talking?" Sam asked. "Look at verse eight."

"Peter."

"Who is Peter talking about?"

Allister read several sentences silently. "Jesus Christ," he answered.

"So Jesus Christ, through His death on a wooden cross and His resurrection three days later, provides us with our salvation, forgiveness of our sins, and eternal life. Going to church or saying prayers doesn't do it. Belonging to a church-going family doesn't do it. Memorizing Bible verses doesn't do it. Even being baptized into a church doesn't do it. Some people give lots of money to a church. But you can't buy eternal life. Only Jesus Christ provides us our salvation, only putting faith in Him gives us eternal life."

Allister's mouth dropped open. *It's as if Sam has read my mind.*

The blast of the steam engine closed their conversation for the time being. As Allister flung straw into the growing golden hill on the hay wagon, he had a lot to think about. *Although I read through the entire New Testament last year, I somehow missed these very verses. Maybe it's because the seventeenth century English of my King James Bible sometimes seems like a foreign language. But now thanks to Sam Pollack, an itinerant pitcher from Ontario, I'm beginning to understand.*

I hope there will be more time to talk with him after supper. I feel like a thirsty man who can't get enough water.

chapter five

Meeting the Master

A llister stopped again at the itinerant's tent after he had completed his evening chores and cared for the crew's teams. "Hello, Sam. Hope it's alright for me to drop by."

"Sure it is, Allister. Come in. The night air's nippy."

Sitting cross-legged on the trampled grassy floor of the tent, Allister pulled his Bible out of his shirt where he had tucked it, wrapped in one of his mother's dish towels. "Sam, could we talk more about what this book says about Jesus? There's a lot I still don't understand."

Sam placed a lit lantern on the ground between them. "You brought your Bible. Good. Find the Gospel of John. In chapter three, Nicodemus, an important person among the Jews, comes to talk to Jesus at night. Look what Jesus says to him in verse three."

"... *Verily, verily, I say unto thee, except a man be born again, he cannot see the kingdom of God,*"[6] Allister read aloud.

"Does Nicodemus understand?"

"No. He asks, 'How can a man be born when he is old?'" Allister laughed. "I would probably have asked Jesus the same question."

"What does Jesus answer him? Look at verses five and six."

"... *Except a man be born of water and the Spirit, he cannot enter into the kingdom of God. That which is born of the flesh is flesh; and that which is born of the Spirit is spirit.*"[7]

"What do you think Jesus is telling Nicodemus?"

"Hmm. Jesus isn't saying that Nicodemus needs another physical birth. Instead, he needs a spiritual one." Allister frowned. *How does that happen? I still don't understand.*

"This whole chapter is so full of God's love for us and how He shows it," Sam said, "but let's focus on verses sixteen through eighteen."

"*For God so loved the world,*" Allister read, "*that he gave his only begotten Son, that whosoever believeth in him should not perish, but have everlasting life. For God sent not his Son into the world to condemn the world; but that the world through him might be saved. He that believeth on him is not condemned: but he that believeth not is condemned already, because he hath not believed in the name of the only begotten Son of God.*"[8]

"Allister, if your father had only one son, would he be willing to sacrifice him to save other people?"

Allister wrinkled his nose and laughed. "My father has five sons."

Sam smiled and repeated, "What would he do if he had only one? Sacrifice him? What do you think most fathers would do?"

"If he had only one? He would refuse to sacrifice that precious son."

"But God did," Sam continued. "Now read verse thirty-six."

Allister slid his finger along the page until he found it and read, "*He that believeth on the Son hath everlasting life: and he that believeth not the Son shall not see life; but the wrath of God abideth on him.*"[9]

Allister remained puzzled. *I think I have always believed there was a Jesus. What am I missing?*

"Find the book of Revelation, Allister. In that book, God gives the disciple John the key to being born again, of having a spiritual birth."

Allister thumbed through the many pages of the New Testament. *That is what I want to know—how to have a spiritual birth.*

"Revelation is the last book in the Bible, Allister."

Sam waited until Allister had found it, then he said, "Verse twenty of chapter three has an important key."

"*Behold, I stand at the door, and knock,*" Allister read, "*if any man hear my voice, and open the door, I will come in to him, and will sup with him, and he with me.*"[10]

"What do you need to do with Jesus?" Sam asked. "What does the Bible say to do?"

"Ask Him in." Suddenly every piece God had been giving Allister for the last four years fell into place. *It isn't a mystery. It doesn't require grand efforts. Having God's forgiveness of sins and obtaining the eternal life He had promised is so simple.*

"Do you want to do it now?" Sam asked. "Ask Jesus in?"

"Yes!"

Sam knelt and Allister did the same.

"Tell God," Sam said, "that you agree with Him about who you are, who you believe in, and who you want in your life."

"Dear God, You are right. I am a sinner," Allister prayed. "I need a Saviour. I believe Your son, Jesus, died for me and my sins. Forgive me of my sins. I ask You, Jesus, into my heart and into my life. Amen."

"Heavenly Father," Sam prayed, "bless Allister with Your Holy Spirit. Help him to understand Your words in Your book and to grow in his faith in You. In Jesus' name, Amen."

Sitting back on his heels, Allister sensed something had definitely happened to him. He felt great joy flooding through his entire body. For the first time in his life, he felt clean in his mind and heart. *So this is what it's like to be born again. I feel like shouting it from the rooftops!*

"Allister, we read God cannot lie. We read that if you ask Him into your life, He will come in. Where is the Lord God in the Spirit of His son, Jesus, now?"

Allister touched his chest over his heart, and his face broke into the widest smile possible.

Sam laughed. "That's right, Allister! Now, may I show you two more passages?"

What? There's more?

"Here, sit beside me," Sam urged.

When Allister had moved over to Sam, the pitcher turned back a few pages in his Bible and read aloud. "*And this is the record, that God hath given to us eternal life, and this life is in his Son. He that hath the Son hath life; and he that hath not the Son of God hath not life. These things have I written unto you that believe on the name of the Son of God; that you may know that you have eternal life, and that ye may believe on the name of the Son of God.*"[11]

"Allister, do you have to guess that you have eternal life?"

27

"No, those verses say I can know." Once again, Allister's jaw dropped. *No more guessing.*

"Sam, I *know* I have eternal life," Allister almost shouted, taking his spiritual father by the shoulders and shaking him.

Laughing joyfully, Sam said, "Welcome into our Heavenly Father's family. When you say you are a Christian, you aren't saying you're part of a specific church or a member of a certain religion. You're saying that you're in a relationship with God through ..."

"His son, Jesus."

"That's right, Allister," Sam said, stifling a yawn and sinking back onto the tent's floor with his Bible open in his lap.

"Sorry, Sam. I'm keeping you up."

"It's more than alright, Allister."

"You said two passages," Allister reminded Sam. "What's the second?"

"Find this one in your Bible," Sam said, pointing at a specific verse in his.

"*But seek ye first the kingdom of God, and his righteousness; and all these things shall be added unto you,*"[12] Allister read. *Wow,* he thought, *that sounds like another promise.*

"It's your responsibility to put God and your relationship with Him first," Sam said. "When you do, He promises to add to your life. He will answer your prayers in His way and in His time."

"Thank you, thank you, Sam, for showing me how to receive Jesus. For the first time, I have hope for my life." Allister wrapped his Bible and tucked it inside his shirt. "Sleep well, Sam."

"You're welcome, Allister. Goodnight."

Entering a darkened house and tiptoeing upstairs, Allister quietly returned his Bible to its place in his box of clothes. He marvelled at the change inside his heart. His despair had vanished. The gray confusion of his mind's eye had been replaced by pure white, like sunlight on newly fallen snow. It was as if he had been scrubbed of every sin, cleansed from all angry thoughts. In those places, joy and hope filled every nook and cranny of his soul.

"Where did you disappear to?" Jim whispered so as not to wake up John.

"The crew camp."

"What were you doing? Playing cards, drinking, gambling?"

Allister chuckled. "No, just the opposite."

"What then?"

"Listening to Sam and God and talking to both."

"It isn't even Sunday. Being so religious is …"

"I am not being religious," Allister interrupted. "I now have a personal relationship with God."

"What?" Jim sat up.

"For the first time, I have hope and help for my life, because I asked Jesus into my heart tonight. Now I have His Spirit in me and life eternal!"

"Uh, if you say so." Jim rubbed his eyes, yawned, and laid back down. "I don't see how that'll change anything." He rolled towards the wall.

In a few minutes, Allister guessed from the slowed rising and falling of his brother's side that Jim was already "counting cows as they passed the gate."

Allister, however, was so thrilled with what had happened to him, it was a long time before he could sleep. *I'm not about to let Jim's doubt ruin my new-found faith.* Phrases Allister had read kept running through his mind. Recalling specifically the last verse Sam had shown him, Allister took great comfort in its message. *If I put God first and live a righteous life, He will take care of my needs.* Reassured about his future, Allister fell into a deep sleep.

———◆———

By the fourth afternoon of the harvest of the McRuers' homesteads, the threshing crew had wrapped things up and moved on. All the grain had been locked up in the bins. Father said that he would haul some of it to the elevators while the brothers went with the threshing crews to complete the harvest of the second bumper crop of the decade. Since Allister and Jim were now almost sixteen, Father said they could go too. The brothers packed their wagon with a tent, blankets, clothes, buckets, and feed for John's horses. Mother snuck in a basin, a bar of soap, and towels. Allister tucked his Bible among his clothes. They didn't need to bring food or cooking gear because the crews were always well fed by the farm families they worked for.

Allister's original dread of this itinerant labour experience disappeared. He was actually looking forward to it because the month of travel from farm to farm would give him time every evening for Sam's able tutoring in Allister's new faith. When Jim tried to get his twin to join a group of the men and teenage boys in some card games, Allister went a couple of times. But he soon refused. The swearing and sleazy stories that seemed to accompany the card playing were now useless chatter and increasingly distasteful to him. At the risk of being teased, Allister spent more and more of his time reading his Bible or studying it with Sam. He felt like a starving soul who couldn't get enough.

At the end of the final itinerant threshing session and their last evening together, Allister had a difficult time saying goodbye to the man he regarded as his spiritual father and mentor.

"Always remember, Allister, you are never alone. You have a very able teacher inside you—the Holy Spirit," Sam said. "Ask Him to help you understand what God's Word says. You will remain in my prayers."

"Thank you, Sam."

"As you learn more about the Lord and God's Word, readily share what you learn with others."

"I will, Sam."

———◆———

After dealing with armies of stooks, wagonloads of bagged grain, mountains of straw, and clouds of grain dust, the four McRuer brothers returned home to find a very worried father. While the warm, dry weather had been good for threshing, Father said it hadn't been good for conditions on Turtle Mountain. He also told them that operations at the saw mill had been temporarily suspended. The reason? The usual fall rains were late and the forest floor was bone dry. Mr. Morton, the mill's owner, had said it'd only take a spark to set off an inferno.

chapter six

Burning Mountain

Worried about the dryness of the timber on Turtle Mountain, Father debated the safety of the farm's remaining stacks of lumber. "Dan, your homestead is on the other side of the road and a good mile north. The dirt road should act like a break. I don't think a fire could jump it. Would it be alright for us to store our lumber at your place until the danger is past?"

"Of course, Father," Dan said. "When do you want to move it?"

"Before we do anything else."

———•———

While waiting for the fall rains to come, Allister and Jim herded the cattle to glean leftover grain in the fields. Dan and John helped Father haul wagon-loads of grain to Cherry Creek and Desford.

After breakfast several mornings later, there was a heated discussion between Father, John, and Dan in the middle of the farmyard. Allister saw his father stomp off in the direction of the barn. John and Dan followed. When Father came out with one of their teams, he didn't return to the usual plowing of additional acres, as he had previously insisted they do "in readiness for winter." Instead, Allister watched in amazement as his father guided his team and plow along the side of the barn.

Puzzled, Allister hurried across the farmyard and into the barn.

"What in the world are you and Father doing, John?" Allister asked while his brothers harnessed the other team. "Surely Father isn't planning on planting a field of wheat right next to the barn."

"No, he isn't. We're plowing fire breaks around the barn and both Father's and my grain bins—just in case."

At last, a line of dark clouds rumbled on the horizon. But before the farmers and loggers could rejoice that the rain had finally come, lightning ricocheted and thunder resounded off the rocks of Turtle's Back, high on Turtle Mountain.

As the clouds churned above their farm, and the lightning flashed, taking cover inside the farmhouse wasn't enough for Jessie's pet, Tawny. One more flash and the Sheltie went missing.

"Tawny! Tawny!" Jessie screamed. She ran through the kitchen, the sitting room, and the dining room, calling for her dog. When she couldn't find her, Jessie sat on the floor and bawled. "I can't find Tawny. She run away."

"Allister, would you help your sister? Search the house," Mother said. "I don't think anyone has let her out."

After checking under and behind everything in the basement and main floor, Allister searched the bedrooms. Minutes later, he called from the top of the stairs. "Found her."

"Where is she?" Mother asked.

"Under Jessie's bed."

"Alright. Just leave her there. Father's calling for you, Allister."

Father, John, Dan, and Jim were standing in a huddle in the farmyard when Allister ran outside. "Look, Allister!" Father exclaimed, pointing up the mountain.

Flames were leaping. The brief shower that had accompanied the lightning strikes had done nothing to slow the fire jumping from tree to tree.

"If that inferno spreads in this direction," John said, "we'll be glad we took the time to plow those firebreaks. Right, Father?"

Ignoring John's remark, Father snapped. "Allister, Jim, Dan, be quick. Get our cattle out of the south pasture. Herd them to Dan's place."

When Allister and his brothers got to the south pasture, however, they were met by an avalanche of fleeing animals. Birds in panicky flight were followed by lunging deer, foxes, coyotes, wolves, bears, skunks, and every other Turtle Mountain creature. Their Angus cattle and Guernsey cow were milling near the gate, rolling their eyes and bawling. When Dan opened the gate, their livestock fled north with the wildlife, away from the encroaching flames.

"Good thing the horses are in the other pasture," Dan said. "We'll need them to round up our cattle."

"Only if John and Father catch them before they jump the fence," Jim said.

Tearing back to the barnyard, the brothers found Father and John trying to handle four frightened horses. "Shalazar's already jumped the fence!" John hollered.

"Let's blindfold the horses and harness them in the barn," Dan suggested. "They'll be easier to handle."

"Dan, you haven't had enough time to move the cattle. Where are they?"

"Already at my place, I expect."

"What do you mean, you expect?"

"They bolted with the mountain animals."

Father groaned. "We may have lost every one of them then."

"And Shalazar," Jim added.

"Allister, Jim, catch any chickens still here. Lock them up in the coop. I'll use Jake and Maggie to move it to the middle of our farmyard. We'll look for our cattle later."

Mother ran out of the house to help catch the chickens. When all the flighty birds within arm's reach had been locked in the coop, Father had Jake and Maggie pull it near the windmill.

Satisfied that the majority of her chickens were in a safer spot, Mother scanned the growing inferno on Turtle Mountain. "We might have to put out some grass fires if they spread closer to our farmyard. Allister, Jim, round up as many burlap sacks as you can find. Put my wash tub outside and fill it with water from the well. The cistern is dry."

As soon as Allister had poured a bucket of water into the tub, Mother dumped sacks in it to soak them.

Smoke billowed and the crackle of flames got closer as the fire dropped from the tree line at the edge of the mountain to the prairie grass and crop stubble not yet plowed under.

"Jim, take the horses over to Dan's place!" Father hollered. "They'll be safer there. Leave them in harness in the barn and get back here."

Grabbing the reins of the other three horses, Jim vaulted onto Jake's back and dug his heels into the draft horse's flanks. Already nervously reacting to the smell of smoke, the teams needed no urging to race north cross-country.

A short time later, Allister heard his mother hollering for help. Everybody ran through the smoky haze to the back of the house to see the grass around the cordwood ablaze. Grabbing two wet sacks out of Mother's tub, Allister worked with everyone, including Jessie, to beat out flames.

"Everyone, over here!" Father yelled, running towards the machine shed.

Whap! Swish, whap! Allister swung his wet sacks, first one and then the other, at the flames. Coughing from the smoke, he ran back to the tub next to the house, dunked his sooty sacks, and grabbed two more from the water. Back and forth he went. So did everyone else.

"Angus, Jim, get more water from the well," Father hollered. "The tub is running out."

Pump, pump, pump. Run and run. Slosh, slosh, slosh, splash. Buckets of water refilled the tub.

"Bring some of those buckets over here," Mother yelled, pointing at the grass around the outhouse.

Minutes later, there was a collective groan.

"Got there too late," John said.

By the time the family had finally succeeded in slapping out or dousing all the flames in the farmyard, the outhouse had burnt to the ground and the machine shed's south wall was scorched. But the house, their winter's supply of firewood, the barn, and Father's grain bins were saved. For a moment, the family stood in the middle of their farmyard coughing, gasping for fresh air, and surveying the sooty scene around them.

"Let's check my homestead," John said. "Bring a soaked sack with you."

Flinging dripping burlaps over his shoulder, Allister ran with his brothers along the road past the schoolhouse to John's place. The fire had circled the bins and run out of fuel at the edge of the road. The brothers beat out smoldering areas near the bins.

"The schoolhouse is next!" Allister shouted.

When they entered the yard, there was a collective groan. The trees along the western perimeter were scorched. The stable and outhouses were piles of ash.

"But it didn't seem to touch the school. Why?" Jim asked.

"The walls are tin sheeting," John explained. "We still need to check the roof. It's wood shingle."

"Whoever was supposed to plow the fire break around the school this year didn't get it done in time," Dan growled.

Trying the schoolhouse door and finding it unlocked, Allister went inside. The room appeared as if teacher and students had dropped everything and fled. *I wonder where they are,* he thought. *Hope everybody is safe.*

When he came outside carrying a ladder, the teacher and her students with their horses were coming back across the road. Allister set the ladder against the schoolhouse wall. Wetting his sack at the pump, he handed it to Dan for him to climb up and inspect the roof.

Allister turned and counted fifteen children gathered in the schoolyard. Somebody tackled him from behind. "Oh hi, Georgie," Allister said. "Is everybody alright?"

"Yes, but ... it looks like Miss Johnson was right," Georgie said.

"Right about what?"

"Our horses. Good thing we took them with us. Look at the stable. Several fathers aren't going to be happy about the buggies the fire burnt up."

"I think they'd rather have that loss than lose any one of their children," Allister said.

"Yeah. Well, Miss Johnson says we'd better put our things away and get home. Says our parents will be worried. Doesn't look like the fire is done, though. Look!"

Georgie and Allister stood for a moment watching the smoke pluming from the top of Turtle Mountain. The wind had shifted, blowing from the east and spreading the flames along the length of the mountain.

"Oh boy, pretty soon there won't be any forest left," Allister said. "Better get home, Georgie. Hope your folks are alright. Your farm is closer to the mountain than ours, and we lost a building."

"You did? Which one?"

"The outhouse."

"The outhouse!" Georgie roared with laughter. Waving goodbye, the boy walked towards the schoolhouse, muttering, "The outhouse!"

———————

"Allister, we need to get our horses and round up our cattle," John said.

"I'll get Tawny," Jim said. "The storm has moved on. There's been no thunder or lightning for some time now. Maybe she's calmed down enough to help us herd."

Riding Maggie, Allister searched the prairie east of Dan's farmyard. Not far away, he found a cluster of the cows. Bessie and two of the Angus cows were standing with their calves tucked behind them, defending their youngsters from a pack of circling wolves. Knowing he couldn't very well chase the menaces off by himself, he turned Maggie around and galloped in search of Dan. "Dan, where's your gun?" Allister hollered when he found his brother. "A pack of wolves has surrounded some of our cattle."

Wheeling Jake around, Dan hollered over his shoulder. "Follow me." At the door to his house, Dan slid to the ground, handed his reins to Allister, and ran inside. In less than a minute, Dan came out with his hunting rifle and a box of ammunition. Handing the box to Allister, Dan swung back up on Jake. "Show me where they are!"

The brothers urged their mounts into a gallop. Within minutes, they were within shooting range.

"Which one is the leader of the pack?" Dan asked.

Allister pointed. "The rest of the pack seem to be following that wolf's lead."

Dan slid off Jake, took a bullet as he handed over the horse's reins, and loaded the gun. Walking a few paces away, Dan knelt on one knee, aimed, and fired. The pack leader yelped and his back legs gave way. In a panic, Dan ran over to Allister. "Missed my mark. Need another bullet."

Dan reloaded, took aim, and fired again. This time the wolf dropped and the others scattered. "Let's get our livestock home before the wolves come back, Allister."

Stuffing the box of bullets in his pants' pocket, Allister rode behind the group of cows. Whistling and swinging a rope, he and Maggie ranged back and forth behind the cows and calves. With Dan on Jake doing the same, the two brothers managed to drive their nervous charges back the way they had come. When Bessie was within sight of the barn, she ran straight for it, mooing as she went. Evidently, she'd had enough of an adventure for one day. Half an hour later, John, Jim, and Tawny drove in two other Angus cows and the bull.

Being short one Angus cow and calf, the brothers and Tawny returned to the search. On the empty claim next to Dan's, the brothers rode along an obvious animal flight path through the prairie grass. Tawny ran ahead, frequently disappearing in the tall grass. Her sharp barking let them know she'd found something. Following the sound to a spot away from the animal trail, they guided their mounts at a trot to a sad scene. Their one remaining Angus cow was standing next to her dead calf. From the torn-up turf and bloody lacerations on her neck and hind legs, the brothers could see the mama had tried to defend her baby even after the coyotes had killed it. When Tawny burst on them, barking ferociously, the coyotes had apparently fled. Now the dog sat next to the dead calf, whimpering.

Allister slid off Maggie and knelt in the grass. Smiling, he stroked Tawny's head. "Good dog!"

"What do we do now?" Jim asked.

"Bring the calf home. Our cow has defended her baby at the risk of her own life. She won't leave without it," John said. "Dan, help me lay it across Jake's back. He's hauled a deer carcass home before, so he'll be the least likely to spook at its smell and dead weight."

When they got back to the barn, Father examined the cow's wounds. He and Mother washed and buttered them.

"What should we do with the calf?" John asked.

"Bury it in the pasture near the barn," Father said. "We don't dare eat it, since wild dogs have bitten into it. Plus we don't know how many hours it's been lying in the sun. It's not safe meat, even for Tawny."

After the injured cow was put into the barn, Father removed the harness from Jake and got on him to ride bareback. "Angus, put his halter on over his bridle, clip a lead rope to it, and hand me the rope."

"Where are you going, Father?" Jim asked.

"To Cherry Creek."

"Why?"

"To get some medicine from the pharmacy for our cow's injuries. We need to make sure they don't get infected."

With that, Father and Jake were down the farm lane at a gallop.

———◆———

After Father left, Dan hitched John's team to the wagon to retrieve some of the lumber at his place. With Mother and Jessie needing the privacy of a privy, John said they must rebuild their outhouse immediately.

Allister joined Mother and Jessie in animal inventory. At last count, their fire losses in livestock were one horse, one calf and … they had yet to count the chickens. One broody hen, two layers, and four pullets were all that were left. "Not to worry, Allister," Mother said. "If a fox or coyote doesn't get them, a few more might straggle back."

———◆———

An hour after dark, Father returned on Jake, leading a second horse. Everyone came out of the house to see what was going on. The horse Father was leading was Shalazar. When Mother came out the back door, she was greeted by several joyous wickers. "Hello, boy," Mother said, stroking her horse. "Did you think we got lost? Where did he turn up, Father?"

"The livery stable in town. While the pharmacist prepared the ointment, I took Jake over to the stable's big water trough. The manager came out and said, 'I believe I've got one of your horses in my paddock. Come have a look.'"

"How did that happen?" Jim asked.

"Well, the guy said the horse just showed up—loose, lathered, and wild eyed, but hung around, wouldn't leave. I told the guy Turtle Mountain is burning and the wildlife fleeing through our farm caused Shalazar to bolt."

"Welcome home, boy," Jim said, patting the horse's neck. Taking his lead rope, Jim led him to the barn.

"This is amazing," Father said. "We've hardly lost anything, and it could've been so much worse. Hope Thomas and his family have done as well."

As Allister finished evening chores, he whispered, "Thank You, Heavenly Father, for Your protection and help today."

chapter seven

Stomping Bricks

Allister thrust his shovel into the mound of light-yellow sand on which he, Jim, and Dan were standing. "Hey, Dan, why does Father want us to make bricks?"

"To give our house a fire-proof veneer."

Jim added his shovelful to the wheelbarrow nearby. "Couldn't Father buy bricks?"

"Maybe," Dan said. "Last winter, I overheard Father and John have several arguments about how to get enough bricks, ever since fire spread from Turtle Mountain and came so close to burning down our home.

"One problem was finding out who had any bricks for sale. When Father asked at the lumber yard in Cherry Creek, he learned the main supplier was a company in New Brunswick."

"New Brunswick? That's over a thousand miles from here," Allister said. "The only feasible way to ship bricks such a distance would be by rail, wouldn't it?"

Dan dropped a shovelful of sand into the wheelbarrow. "Yes. Father said the cost of the freight alone would be a fortune. Probably one of the reasons he decided we should try to make our own. John did ask around. He told me some of the local farmers have taken up brick-making recently."

"Really? Which farmers? Where?"

"Near Whitewater, Killarney, and Ninga."

"Ninga?" Jim chimed in. "That's close. I don't see why Father doesn't just buy bricks from that farmer."

"I agree," Allister said. "Making so many bricks will be a tremendous amount of work."

"Father insists that buying enough bricks to cover the walls of the house would cost too much money," Dan said. "To quote Father, 'Why pay out even a penny when we can get clay for free?' And it's probably the same clay the Ninga fellow is using."

"I thought bricks had to be fired." Allister paused his shovelling. "Where's the kiln?"

"John said he's going to build it over at his place. Mother's afraid Jessie or Tawny might accidently burn themselves if we build it here." Dan laid his shovel on top of the load of sand. "Good thing Father discovered this hill of sand. Since it was under only a thin layer of topsoil and is close to our farmhouse, it was easy to get to and we don't have far to lug it. You two grab the handles and I'll show you where to deposit this load. Then get four more while I help Father and John dig the pit for the clay stomping."

After breakfast several days later, Mother and Jessie packed a crate of food and gear for camping. John came into the kitchen with a rolled-up blanket. "Allister, Jim, Father says you're to come with us. Joe promised to come and help Mother and Jessie with chores while we're gone. Better bring a change of clothes as well as your blanket. It's pretty dirty work."

When Allister ran outside with his blanket roll, Dan and Father were pitching a layer of sand into the bed of both Father's and John's wagons.

"Allister, Jim, get as many empty burlap sacks as you can find," Father said. "Jim, better bring several buckets and a couple of sacks of feed for our teams too."

After he had done what his father asked, Allister walked over to where John was putting a collection of tools into his wagon.

"Allister, don't just stand there," John said. "Locate three poles we can use as a tripod for our cooking pot while I load some firewood. We won't be able to find either out on the prairie."

Once everything necessary was loaded, Father directed his wagon cross-country to Dan's claim. After skirting around fields green with growing oats and wheat, Father and John drove their teams almost straight north to the stream bank known for its quality clay.

When they reached the prairie near the stream, John picked a spot for their campsite. Everyone searched along the bank to find some rocks for a campfire ring while Father unharnessed and hobbled the horses to turn them out to graze. John dug up the earth under their campfire spot. They completed the rock ring, built a firewood tipi in the middle of it, and set up a tripod for hanging a pot over their fire.

With their camp set up, Father set everyone to work cutting two-to-three-pound chunks of the light, gray clay from the stream bank below their camp. Allister grunted as he pushed while Jim pulled their burlap sacks of chunks up the bank and dumped the clay on the ground behind a wagon. At the end of each struggle up the bank, Allister realized, a bit late, that his efforts to wipe away his sweat meant he had been smudging clay all over his face and neck. Glancing around at his father and brothers, he could see they had been doing the same thing. They would all look like gray ghosts shortly.

An hour before sunset, Father stopped their work. "That's enough for today," he said, spreading some of the sacks over the large mound of clay. "Dan and Jim, wet down the sacks. Must keep the clay moist. We'll load it tomorrow."

John handed Allister a stick with a string and a small hook. "Let's go fishing," he said, showing some wiggly worms he'd dug up.

Allister grinned. He was delighted to be invited.

John removed his clay-caked boots and waded into the cool stream.

Allister needed no urging to copy his brother. *What I want most of all is to take a dip. To get completely free of my coating of gray dust.* "John, let's go out a little further."

"Alright, but be careful. Sometimes streams have drop offs, like the one near Killarney. Remember how to float?"

"Hope so," Allister said as he waded out and down the stream. When the water was up to his hips, he dunked himself and sat on its silt bottom a while. The gently flowing water cooled him, washing the clay away. He wiggled his toes. *Ah! This is wonderful.*

Seconds later, Allister jumped up. *Something was nibbling at my toes!*

"Ready to fish now?" John asked.

Allister and John hooked worms, cast their bait, and waited. It wasn't long before they had a couple of trout.

When they got back to their camp, a fire crackled in its stone circle. A pot of water boiled over the flames. Allister changed into his dry clothes, draped the wet ones on a bush to dry, and helped John gut their catch. From bushes growing along the stream's bank, Dan cut sticks on which to grill their fish. Father and Jim laid a few logs near the campfire. Then they all sat, salivating at the smell of their fresh catch cooking. Supper was fish, scones, and cups of hot tea with a pinch of sugar.

After they'd eaten, John doused the rocks around the fire with water from the stream. Steam rose from the heated side of the rocks. An extra bucket of water sat nearby in case the fire jumped out of the ring.

Calling their horses and rattling some feed in a bucket, Dan waited for them to come before pouring four equal amounts on the ground near the wagon. While the horses were munching their grain, John and Father hauled water for them, and Jim tethered them to their wagons for the night.

Laying their blankets on the ground around the campfire, father and sons were soon quiet. Allister stared up at the stars for a few moments but was tired enough to leave the buzzing of the few early mosquitoes and the songs of the prairie's cicadas and crickets unheard.

Dawn on the open prairie was greeted by the meadowlarks and whippoorwills. Allister tried but didn't succeed in sleeping through their morning welcome. Rising and stretching, he looked around for an appropriate place to use as nature's outhouse. Their horses stood with heads drooping and eyes closed. His business completed, Allister took a bucket and slid down the slippery bank to the stream to get some water for the horses.

He surprised a deer at the stream's edge. Leaping through the water, the startled doe fled over the opposite bank. Allister watched her graceful flight until all he could see was the bouncing white of her flag of a tail.

"Isn't she beautiful?" A voice exclaimed from behind Allister. Turning around, he smiled in agreement.

Jim had been watching too. "Father says the old timers watched herds of buffalo on these prairies."

"Too bad they're gone."

"Maybe. But we wouldn't like them in Mother's corn or our wheat and oat fields." Jim dipped a pot into the stream. "John says breakfast will be ready soon. I'll feed the horses if you'll water them."

———

Joining his father and brothers, Allister drank hot tea and ate biscuits Mother had packed. Dipping spoons into the pot of oatmeal, they polished off the porridge in no time.

After breakfast, they began the day's work of cutting more chunks of clay and building a mound behind the other wagon. By noon, they had enough to fill both wagons.

After dinner break, Allister harnessed the teams, packed up camp, and drowned the fire while his father and brothers loaded the clay.

Father's method was a little strange. Standing behind a wagon, Father and John stretched a piece of sack between them. Dan shovelled a chunk onto the sack. Swinging the sack between them, Father and John flung the lump into the back of the wagon. Jim stood in the wagon and rolled the clay lumps towards the front. Soon the shovel, swing, plop, roll assembly line had loaded both mounds of clay.

During their trip back, everyone walked. The McRuers' homesteads were at the foot of Turtle Mountain and uphill from the stream's bank of clay deposits. The teams had a hard enough time pulling the wagons with their heavy loads. Allister's back soon ached from pushing the wagons from time to time.

Once home, Father and John backed their wagons up to the pit they had dug before the trip. Father, John, and Dan hoed and shovelled the loads into the pit. It was Allister and Jim's job to take care of the teams before doing their regular evening chores. When they walked past the clay pit to the house, they saw that both wagons were empty and the mound of clay was covered with wet sacks.

The next morning while Allister, Jim, and Jessie did morning chores, John, Dan, and Father built brick boxes or forms.

"Jim, Allister, Dan, take off your shoes and stomp into the clay the water and sand we have added," Father said. "Jessie, go get Mother. We need her help too."

"Better roll up our pant legs," Allister suggested.

The cold squish of the clay between his toes reminded Allister of his dunk in the stream during their trip. The feeling was strange, but good. When Father and John poured water or shovelled sand into the pit, the texture of the mush changed.

While the brothers stomped, Mother and Jessie spread sand in the parts of farmyard that had full sun. Tawny followed Jessie around most of the time. Sometimes the little Sheltie sat and watched the stomping.

"I bet the dog is wondering what in the world we're doing." Allister laughed.

"She probably thinks we've gone crazy," Jim said.

When Father and John thought the consistency of the mixture was just right, father and sons rolled "loaves" of it in sand, plopped the loaves into the wooden forms, levelled the top of each form, and dumped the "bricks" out onto a patch of sanded ground. Mother and Jessie's job was to stand the bricks up side by side so they could dry in the hot sun.

It was hot, thirsty, muddy work. Dinner time and breaks to drink or douse himself with cool well water were a welcome relief to Allister. With hour upon hour of the stomping, his legs ached more and more. What seemed easy at the beginning became increasingly exhausting.

Before their second trip for more clay, the bricks they had made and sun-dried were loaded into the wagons, hauled to John's homestead, and stacked in his kiln for firing.

The short break the family took for the Dominion Day celebrations was followed by two months of constant brick making. Camping trips to gather more clay, days to stomp and pack bricks were balanced with garden tilling, tree watering, and haying. There seemed an endless supply of farm chores and building projects.

Brickmaking had to be put on hold with the arrival of the harvest season. Allister had already helped Dan, John, and Father with their oat harvests. The week Wood Lake School reopened to start the new school year, Allister was driving a team pulling John's brand-new McCormick reaper across his wheat field. Enjoying the ease with which the machine did what had been back-breaking work for him, Allister focused on the sweeps across the golden acres, unaware of how close he was getting to the schoolyard.

"Allister! Wait a minute!"

He stopped the horses and turned in his seat to see who was hollering at him. It was Georgie. His young friend was no longer a little boy.

Allister climbed down and unhitched the team to let them know they could rest a bit. Leading them near the edge of the field, he greeted the boy. "Long time, no see, Georgie," Allister said. "You're growing like those weeds in your pa's wheat fields!"

"Ha, ha! Didn't know you were such a comic! You're no shorty, either, for your information. How tall are you now?"

"Taller than Father," Allister said with a grin. "What grade are you in?"

"Fifth."

"What's your teacher's name?"

"Miss Hill."

"That means you've had a different teacher for every year you've been in school."

"Guess so."

"What's your favourite subject so far? And don't tell me dinner break or recess."

"Nature study."

"That's new, isn't it? Did your teacher last year teach that subject?"

"No, but this one is. Right now we're learning about bugs. She has us collecting them for displays."

"Then here's one for your collection."

Allister grabbed a grasshopper from a prairie grass stem nearby and handed the squirming critter to the boy. Georgie dropped the insect into his pants' pocket and held it shut so the bug couldn't escape.

"Georgie, would you do me a favour? Find out if Miss Hill has a high school education and then come tell me after school on your way home."

"How do I find out?"

"Ask her, but don't tell her or anyone why you're asking. Be our secret, alright?"

"Sure," Georgie said, grinning. "See you later."

Hitching John's team to the reaper once more, Allister resumed the task of cutting and bundling the wheat in his brother's field. Although Allister hadn't brought up the subject with his parents during the past two years, he hadn't forgotten his decision to become a doctor or his plan to go to high school.

I'm not sure how much longer I'll have to wait. If I can just find a teacher who has completed high school herself, she might be able to tutor me through the ninth-grade subjects, at least. Then perhaps I could sit for the June exams at the Cherry Creek High School.

The trouble was that all of the teachers at Wood Lake School so far had been young men and women with no more than Grade 8. And most of these had gotten their education in a one-room schoolhouse just like the one on the corner acre of his father's homestead.

As the afternoon wore on, Allister finished the binding and joined John and Jim in the stooking process. Turning from time to time to look at the schoolhouse, Allister bent and lifted the bound bundles of grain to make row upon row of golden pyramids.

By the time the three of them had stooked half way across the field, Allister saw the children pour out of the schoolhouse, and Georgie run towards him. *At last. Is he going to tell me that I can get help to continue my studies from this new teacher?* With a lump of anticipation in his throat, Allister forced himself to continue stooking and stopped only when the boy was standing next to him.

"Allister, I asked Miss Hill the question you told me to ask her," Georgie said. "She said no, she didn't go to high school."

"Alright, Georgie. Thanks for asking her. You'll remember to keep our secret, won't you? Study hard! Learn all about those bugs and everything else you can!"

"Alright. See you later. I'd better get home. Got stooking to do too, Allister."

"Aargh! The golden monsters chase us farm boys in our nightmares!"

Georgie's laughter bounced across the field as he headed for the trail running west along the foot of Turtle Mountain towards his home.

Allister's hope for a mental reprieve from boredom now fluttered to the ground. *Looks like I'll have to wait another year,* he thought. *I'm so glad I've got my relationship with You, Lord Jesus. Got some growing to do, I know. Especially when it comes to having patience.*

The hour Allister could spend reading and studying his Bible was the one portion of each day he relished. Although he'd tried to explain to each member of his family about his newfound relationship with his Heavenly Father and the joy that God's presence in his life was bringing him, no one except his mother understood. The others just wondered out loud, from time to time, why Allister spent so much time reading his Bible and why he seemed like a new person—someone at peace, a hard worker, a teenager whose temper no longer ruled him.

chapter eight

Rescuing Hope

Allister stood on the top plank of a scaffold Father and John had built along the front of the family farmhouse. Out of the corner of his eye, Allister glimpsed a boy running towards him from the schoolyard at the end of the first day of the new school year.

When he took a second look, he recognized his young friend, Georgie. Allister put aside his trowel of mortar and the yellow brick he was holding. *Wonder if he has the good news I have been waiting for—a teacher who can help me continue my studies.*

"Hey, Allister, got a minute?" the boy called, acting a bit out of breath.

"Sure, Georgie." Allister looked at his twin who was on the scaffold with him. "Be right back, Jim."

After climbing down, Allister asked. "Alright, Georgie, what is it?"

The boy backed away from the house, and Allister followed.

Looking at the scaffold as if to make sure they were far enough away to be out of earshot, Georgie asked, "Remember our secret? The question you told me to ask my teacher?"

When Allister nodded, the boy whispered. "We have another new teacher this year. Her name is Miss Thompson. She's a recent graduate of Cherry Creek High School."

"Georgie, that's wonderful news!" Allister slapped his young friend on the back. Then he whispered, "Maybe I can come to school this fall. But it'll have to be after harvest. Please keep this our secret for now."

Allister went back to laying brick, and Georgie ran off.

"What was that all about?" Jim asked from his end of their row of laid bricks.

"Tell you later."

———

One noon in early October, Allister returned from delivering a wagon-load of grain to the elevator in Desford. *Today is the day. I must ask today if I am to return to school Monday next. I have waited long enough.*

On the kitchen table, Allister laid the family's mail and newspaper he had fetched from their Desford postbox. Surprised to find John manning the stove again, Allister asked, "Where's Mother?"

He was fairly sure he shouldn't bring up the subject of more schooling if she wasn't home.

"She went to see Sofi Dirksen," John said as Father and Jim entered the house.

"Sofi Dirksen?" Father grumped. "She doesn't even speak English."

"Sofi had her baby several days ago," John said. "Because this is Sofi's fourth child, Mother's concerned. She said she thinks Sofi might need some help. Mother promised to be back by supper."

After Father said the blessing, John continued. "Dan told me that Sofi and her family have only been in Manitoba about six months."

"Where'd they come from?" Allister asked.

"The Ukraine," John said. "Mother says that it must have been very hard on Sofi to travel so far, pregnant, with so many small children."

"Yeah, I suppose so," Father mumbled, his mind obviously elsewhere. "Allister, how did the grain sale go?"

Father's got a one track mind, Allister thought. "Different agent today. The man tested every sack. All came out top grade." He held out the bill of sale and money.

Father looked at the slip of paper, counted the money, and stuffed both in a pants' pocket. "Thanks, son."

Since my first harvest as a full-time farmer three years ago, Allister thought, *Father's, John's, and Dan's homesteads have been doing well, as far as*

I can see. Even then, Father makes it sound like he and his farm are hard up! Not sure why. Guess I'd better wait 'til Mother gets home to reopen the discussion on any further education.

———◆———

After supper, Father stayed in the kitchen reading the newspaper and sipping a cup of tea. Before Mother and Jessie started doing the dishes, Allister said he needed to talk about something important.

When he had both of his parents' attention, he said, "I want to return to Wood Lake School next Monday to continue my studies."

With raised eyebrows, Father dropped his paper.

"Why, son? I thought you had finally settled into farming. You've seemed at peace, almost happy for the past two years."

"You spent a lot of time with that crew member, Sam," Mother said. "I thought those conversations helped you."

"Yes, they did, Mother. What I learned from Sam helped me deal with my disappointment at not being able to get more schooling. And now, I think it's time for me to continue my studies. I've just heard the new teacher is a high school graduate. I won't have to leave home to do the ninth grade!"

Mother turned towards Father. "At least let Allister try. John and Jim are here. Dan isn't far away. We have enough money to buy any additional equipment or horses we need."

"Alright, son, you can study over the winter," Father conceded. "But in the spring, I'll expect you back in the fields. You probably won't make much progress. I've heard ninth grade is no picnic."

At last! Thank you, Lord, for helping him to change his mind. Allister couldn't help smiling from ear to ear. "Thank you, Father. I will do my best."

With that, Father disappeared behind his paper.

Allister got up quickly, gave Mother a peck on the cheek, and returned the hug Jessie had wrapped him in. Sitting on the boot bench next to the back door, Allister ducked his head so his father wouldn't see the tears of joy wetting the corners of his eyes. *Finally, a chance to take the first step towards a high school education. No more waiting. Wonder what subjects ninth graders study.*

———◆———

The next morning, Mother invited Allister to go with her and Jessie for a return trip to Sofi's Soddy. "Bring a saw, the metal wedge, and an axe," she said. "While Jessie and I help Sofi, I want you to split some firewood and kindling for her. I saw no sign of her husband or his tools yesterday."

After Allister loaded the tools in the back of his mother's buggy, he harnessed and hitched Shalazar. Tying the horse to the ring at the back door, Allister loaded the supplies his mother handed to him before he helped her into the buggy. When he lifted Jessie in, Tawny whined to be lifted into it too. Jessie's pet loved buggy rides.

"You drive, Allister," Mother said. "The Dirksens have temporarily occupied the old Smith place, one of the claims that had been abandoned by the time we came to Manitoba."

"Umm … I vaguely remember. Better give me specific directions when we're close."

Allister reined Shalazar westward onto the road to Desford.

"I don't doubt that you can do the ninth grade, Allister," Mother said as their horse trotted along. "Try to understand your father. School was hard for him. He believes it's the same for you. Then too, every father wants his son to follow in his footsteps."

"Four of his sons have, Mother," Allister said. "Isn't that enough?"

"Turn here. The sod house is tucked into the ravine's bank way over there." Mother pointed. "I've brought some food. When Jessie and I came to visit yesterday, there wasn't very much in the Dirksens' house." Mother's forehead wrinkled with worry lines. "Sofi probably didn't have the energy to put in a garden."

"She might have had to help her husband plant and harvest their crop," Allister suggested. "From what you've told me, they've got no sons or relatives to help."

"Oh, I hadn't thought of that." Mother sighed. "Poor dear. And I thought we had it tough when we arrived."

"It's perfectly possible that her husband hired himself out somewhere after he got his crop harvested. This family probably spent all their money just getting here."

The foot path their buggy was following wound down a steep slope and around a scrubby oak. Stopping next to it, he was amazed to find himself in front of a house. It had been dug into the side of the hill. Its roof blended with the grassy thatch that covered the incline. A small window on each side of the door, and a wooden washtub leaning against the Soddy's wall, were the only other evidences of a home.

At the sound of Tawny's excited barking and Mother's hello, three tiny, stair-step girls ran out. They gathered around Jessie and Mother as they climbed down.

When Tawny jumped out of the buggy, the littlest girl ran around her sisters and away from the dog.

"Don't be afraid," Mother said.

"Tawny won't hurt you," Jessie said. "You can pet her. See?" Jessie stroked her dog's head and back.

The biggest girl came over and petted Tawny. After some hesitation, the other two did too.

Tawny wagged her tail.

"She likes you," Jessie said.

Then the three girls caught sight of Allister. Gathering around him, they stared up at him with wide eyes. Shalazar's reins still in his hand, Allister dropped to one knee in the dirt. Pointing at himself, he said, "Allister ... Allister McRuer."

"A-lice," the eldest girl stammered. "Alice."

"No," Allister said, shaking his head. Trying to correct her, he repeated, "Al-li-ster. Allister."

"Al-lis-sir," the girl tried again.

Allister shrugged his shoulders and laughed, a little frustrated. "Allister," he said again. Pointing at the girl, he asked, "What's your name?"

"Lucy," she said. "D-d-dat Hilda," the girl stammered, pointing at the bigger of the other two girls. "See ... see ... sis ... er."

"She is your sister?" he guessed.

Lucy nodded and pointed at the littlest girl. "Dat Greta."

"I'm glad to meet you," he said.

"Hilda, Greta," their mother called from the door of the Soddy.

Allister unhitched Shalazar and led him to the paddock in front of an open-sided shelter. Removing the horse's bridle, Allister turned the gelding loose.

When he saw the paddock's water trough was empty, Allister picked up the one bucket sitting nearby.

"Come," Lucy said, leading the way to a slow trickling stream.

After Allister made sure Shalazar had enough to drink, he followed Lucy to the door of her home. Inside, he saw a short woman wearing a long, black apron over a light blue dress. Her blonde hair was covered with a white cap, its ties hanging loose. When he entered, the woman bent over a wooden cradle to pick up a tiny bundle. As she stooped, Allister noticed the woman's one long, neat braid that ran down her back.

Holding her infant out to Mother, the woman said, "Velcome. I ... Sofi ... You?"

"Allister."

"Alice?"

Oh no, here we go again. Allister shook his head. "Al-li-ster," he repeated slowly.

"Allister," she said.

"That's right. Hello, I'm glad to meet you, Sofi." Allister put out his hand and Sofi smiled as she shook it. He pointed at the empty wood box. "I'll split some wood."

He sniffed the smoky air inside the Soddy. It smelled like a strange mixture of damp earth, boiling coffee, and burnt dung. *Sofi must be burning cow chips.*

Outside, he took his tools over to a pile of old logs behind the shed. *They won't make the greatest cordwood, but they'll burn better than the dung.* He wondered which member of this poor family had scoured the prairie looking for those brown "pies." Since Sofi's cook stove was about one third the size of their stove at home, he sawed the logs into very short lengths. Setting a piece on the chopping block, Allister tapped his wedge into one end with the back of his axe. Then he swung the back of the axe against the wedge with all his might. Crack! The piece of log split in half.

Tap, tap, crack! Tap, tap, crack! Soon a neat pile of firewood was ready for Sofi's cook stove. Using the same process, Allister split one piece of firewood into a bunch of kindling.

Before he had finished splitting all the short lengths of log, Jessie stopped next to him. She shouldered a wooden yoke with buckets hanging from either end. Tawny was close behind her. "Mother says for you to help me fill these buckets. Then it's dinner time."

Allister put his tools in the back of their buggy. *Gotta keep these tools away from tiny fingers.*

After helping Jessie with the water buckets, Allister returned to the stack of wood. Gathering an armload of firewood and kindling, he carried it into the Soddy and dumped the pieces into Sofi's wood box.

The fragrance of Mother's chicken soup permeated the Soddy this time, causing Allister's mouth to water. Three little girls and Jessie were already sitting cross-legged on the dirt floor, sipping hot soup from tin cups and eating biscuits. Each of Sofi's girls asked for more and ate as if they hadn't eaten since yesterday.

After Allister, Sofi, and Mother had also eaten their soup and biscuits, Mother pulled some Alberta apples and raspberry tarts out of her basket. Soon juiced chins and raspberry lips had Sofi saying with smiles and tears in her eyes, "Danke, danke."

Rinsing two tin cups, Sofi filled them with coffee and offered one to Allister.

He didn't really like coffee because of its bitter taste. His family usually drank tea. But his parents had taught him it was impolite to refuse any food or drink offered. "Yes, thank you, Sofi."

Allister took the hot drink and politely sipped it. Mother did the same.

Reaching for one more item she had brought along, Mother thrust Jessie's old coat into Sofi's hands, along with a spool of thread. "Winter's coming. Your girls need warm clothes. Cut this and sew coats for them." Mother pantomimed cutting and sewing as she spoke.

"Ya, danke." Sofi smiled and nodded.

Mother picked up her empty basket and pot. "Jessie, Allister, we'd better be going."

Allister looked around the room one last time. A bed, a table, a stove, a rocking chair, a barrel, and a shelf on the wall made a home of bare essentials for their new friends. But Allister also noticed that a bin of flour, a shaker of salt, some eggs, potatoes, carrots and onions, a canning jar of beef, two jars of tomatoes, and two jars of milk now lined the shelf. Allister silently blessed his thoughtful mother for her warmhearted generosity.

Mother waited until they were well on their way home and out of earshot before she gave a sigh of relief. "Whew! Sofi and her children look much better today."

"Why? What do you mean? Was Sofi sick when you came yesterday?"

"No, I don't believe so. But she was in bed with the baby. The fire was out and the house was chilly, damp, and a mess. It smelled of dirty baby diaper. The little girls were unattended, dirty, thirsty, and very hungry. Jessie and I worked very hard helping Sofi. In fact, Jessie and I were the ones who taught Lucy how to find and burn the cow chips."

"I wondered who had," Allister said. "Our Heavenly Father must've prompted your visit yesterday. Just like the winter Joe was so sick; help arrived just in time for them."

As they continued east along the main road, Mother asked, "Allister, *why* do you want to go to high school?"

"It's the first step to becoming a physician."

"Oh my!" Mother gasped. "That's a tremendous goal!"

"Please don't mention this to anyone just yet, especially Father. Jim and John know I don't want to farm and that I *do* want more education, but that's all I've told them."

chapter nine

Stalemate

Monday morning, Allister joined the children in the yard of Wood Lake School. Georgie was excited to see him. A few of the older students remembered him too. At almost eighteen years of age and six feet tall, he looked more like a parent than a student.

When Miss Thompson came out to ring the bell, she looked at Allister, frowned, and called her regular students to order.

Allister couldn't help sizing her up. *Tall girl. A recent graduate of high school, Georgie said. That means this teacher is probably a year younger than me. Hope she was a good student. I've been out of school for three years now. I'll need lots of help to tackle those ninth-grade studies.*

Once everyone was inside the schoolhouse, Miss Thompson ignored Allister completely.

Picking the biggest desk in the back of the room, Allister tried to get comfortable. Impossible! With his knees sticking into the aisles on both sides, he barely managed to sit in it. He took his supplies out of his book bag and placed them in his desk.

The teacher led the students through their opening exercises and gave them all instructions, subject by subject, grade by grade. But still she said not a word to Allister.

At recess, Allister went outside with the other students. Some of the older boys invited him to play football. Using a blown-up beef bladder as a ball, the boys formed two teams. Soon both sides wanted Allister on their team because of his size and strength.

Recess ended with the clang of the school bell, and everyone returned to their work ... all except Allister. He had none. He sat and waited. *Heavenly Father, why is she ignoring me?*

Dinner break came. Leaving his supplies in his desk and his book bag on it, Allister trudged home with his hands in his pockets. *Until today, I thought my father was my biggest obstacle to an education. I never dreamt a teacher could be.*

When he got home, Allister was relieved to see Mother and Jessie were the only ones there. *At least now I can talk to someone about my dilemma.*

On seeing Allister's face, his mother asked, "What happened?"

"Nothing yet. Miss Thompson ignored me the whole morning. She acted as if I wasn't even there."

"What are you going to do?"

"Wait for her to acknowledge my presence. I am not going to leave before she agrees to give me what I went to the schoolhouse for—help to study ninth-grade subjects! Until today, it hadn't occurred to me that a *teacher*, of all people, would stand in the way of a person wanting to learn!"

At one o'clock, Allister returned to the schoolhouse and his desk. The afternoon crept on. Lessons ended. Miss Thompson wrote out homework assignments on the board for every grade. Then she dismissed the students. All the children picked up their dinner pails and left the schoolhouse.

Still the teacher hadn't spoken to Allister.

He didn't move. *I am not leaving until I've got what I came for.* He prayed, *Heavenly Father, please change this teacher's attitude.*

After Miss Thompson cleaned the blackboard, she settled into her chair at her desk to correct scribblers and make lesson plans for the next day. She continued to ignore Allister.

He sat with jaw set, arms folded across his chest, and his gaze on Miss Thompson. *I've already waited three years to get help with the ninth grade. I can certainly wait a little longer. I am NOT leaving until this teacher agrees to help me.*

An hour passed. Allister continued to wait and pray the teacher would change her mind about him.

Finally, the teacher looked up from her desk and acted startled when she saw Allister hadn't left. "Alright, young man, who are you? And what do you want?"

The tension in Allister's jaw released. He rested his forearms on the desk in front of him and leaned towards the teacher. "My name is Allister McRuer. I graduated from the eighth grade at this school in June of 1895. This year, I want to study the ninth grade here."

The teacher sat, looking stunned for a moment. Allister was sure he could almost hear something similar to the whir of a threshing belt turning rapidly in her head.

Rising, she reached into an extra bookcase she had stuffed next to the blackboard. Carrying a huge pile of books across the room, she plopped them on the desk in front of him. "In that case, you'll need these."

He gulped, but thought, *Steady now, Allister. If she is trying to scare you into giving up your plan, don't let her succeed.*

She brought a chair and set it next to his desk. "Let's start with botany, the study of plants."

Taking the book from the pile and opening to its first chapter, Allister leafed through several pages. Then he wrote in his scribbler the reading assignment and questions the teacher dictated to him.

"Next, let's look at the algebra book," she said.

This was Allister's first exposure to a very different kind of math. He tried to listen but found himself getting confused. But again, he wrote down the homework assignment.

"And oh yes, read the first chapter of the US history text by tomorrow morning." Without another word, she returned to her desk.

Allister gathered his supplies, assignments, and the three textbooks. He put the rest in his desk and started for the door. Before leaving the schoolhouse, he turned back.

With her eyebrows raised, the teacher looked up from her desk.

"Thank you," he said.

Miss Thompson gave him a curt nod but not a glimmer of a smile. "Come at least a half hour before the regular school day starts so I can give you the rest of the homework."

Allister left at a trot. *I'd better hurry*, he thought. *I have chores to do before supper.*

After supper, Allister lit the kerosene lamp on the dining room table and faced the avalanche of ninth-grade learning. While he was trying to make sense of the math, Jim stuck his head over Allister's shoulder. "What kind of arithmetic is that?"

"Algebra!"

"Understand it?'

"Not yet."

"What's this?" Jim picked up the botany text.

"My first science course. Botany, a study of plants."

"Well, you've been a farmer for years. Probably already know a lot about that subject. American History? Why study it?"

"They're our neighbours to the south. Why shouldn't we know about them?"

"How much of that thick book are you supposed to read tonight?"

"About twenty pages, I think."

"Looks like you'll be studying 'til daybreak! Sure you want to do this?"

"Absolutely!"

"Well, good luck!"

An hour later, Mother came into the dining room and sat next to Allister. "Looks like you got what you went for. How long did the teacher make you wait?"

"A full hour past school dismissal."

"Hmm. Wonder what that was all about."

"Don't have a clue."

chapter ten

Sudden Breakthrough

At rooster's crow the next day, Allister was up and out to do his share of chores before breakfast. By eight o'clock, he was ready to leave for school.

"Why so early?" Mother asked.

"Think I'll help Miss Thompson with the schoolhouse's fire every morning. If I help her, maybe she'll be more willing to help me. Besides, she said to come early to get the rest of the assignments."

"Better take my key then. The teacher might not be there this early."

When Miss Thompson arrived at 8:30, Allister had already brought in extra firewood and lit the barrel stove. His homework for botany and algebra lay on her desk, and he was hard at work on a review of his algebra. He'd stumbled through the homework problems and was fairly sure he'd done them incorrectly.

As soon as she had taken off her coat and put away her dinner pail, Miss Thompson called him to her desk. She was smiling. "Allister, thank you for starting the fire. It was a pleasant surprise to enter a warm schoolhouse."

"You're welcome. I'll be happy to light the stove every morning if you would like me to."

"That would be great! Thank you."

Miss Thompson's smile turned into a frown when she pointed at Allister's algebra homework. Repeating the instruction she'd given him yesterday, she wrote examples on the board this time. Twenty minutes later, he had a much better grasp of the basic concept behind this new kind of math. Then the teacher quizzed him on his history reading assignment. Since he had obviously finished it, she assigned questions at the end of the chapter for him to write the answers to. When the teacher glanced at his written homework for botany, she looked surprised.

At nine o'clock, she stood up and handed him several pages of additional assignments from the other texts in his desk. "Well, you've made a surprising start. You'll have to redo the algebra. It's all wrong. Excuse me now. I have to call in the children."

After opening exercises, Allister tackled the algebra problems again and studied the next part of the chapter. From the way things were going with this subject, he figured he'd better try to understand it rather than just memorize formulas. That was the way he'd handled arithmetic in the past, but his method wasn't working with this kind of math.

Getting out the additional texts, he discovered he had reading assignments in geography, literature, bookkeeping, English grammar, French, and agriculture, and a two-page composition to write on one of two topics.

Since the composition wasn't due until next week, Allister set it aside to look at the chapter titles of the book on agriculture. Fruit trees? Raising field and silage corn for dairy cows? What part of Canada was this text based on? Scanning through the information on the title page, he finally found its source—Ontario. *How can this information possibly benefit a farm boy on the Manitoba prairies?* Allister had lived on a farm in Quebec before assisting his parents and brothers on four farms here in Manitoba. From those experiences, he knew the two locations had very different soil resources and weather conditions. *Oh well, if I'm going to be tested on it,* he thought, *I'd better study it anyway. Won't hurt to know more.*

Next he opened the French text. Since he already spoke conversational French, the first two lessons were a snap. Flipping through the pages to get an idea of its quantity of vocabulary and grammar, he figured it might take him a month to complete the entire text.

Intrigued by the idea of learning some bookkeeping, he opened that book next. *If I ever run a business, I will definitely need this information. In fact, it wouldn't hurt for Mother and Jim to learn it with me. This subject I'll do as regular homework at home,* he thought. *Every farm is a business.*

Scrunching over a desk for several hours had put a crick in his back and neck. Allister fidgeted. Rubbing his cramped muscles didn't seem to help. Finally, he stood up, stretched, and went out to the pump for a drink. *Maybe John can help me do something about the desk situation,* he thought. After three years of constant physical activity all day long, Allister found it difficult to adjust to long hours of sitting. *Well, when it gets too hard, I'll go outside with a book and read out loud while I walk, even if others might think I'm crazy. In fact, I think I could read during my walk home and back at dinner break.*

So at noon, Allister grabbed his geography book and finished most of his reading assignment by one o'clock.

At the end of the school day, Allister handed in the reworked algebra assignment, his French, US history, and geography assignments, and the first English grammar work—a two-page listing of nouns and verbs he knew. Miss Thompson's mouth dropped open.

Picking up his literature, agriculture, and bookkeeping homework, he walked home with his nose buried in the literature text. He looked up from the page to make sure he didn't miss the turn off the main road onto the McRuer's farm lane. *At first, this dive into so much study was a bit overwhelming. My brain hasn't had to work so hard for such a long time. My mental muscles need to get stronger. It looks like they'll get plenty of exercise this year.* He grinned.

After late afternoon chores and supper, Allister lit the lamp on the dining room table and invited Jim and Mother to join him during his bookkeeping lesson.

"What's bookkeeping?" Jim asked. "Why do you want us to study it with you?"

"It has to do with keeping accurate records of money earned and spent." Allister pointed at the first page of his textbook. "Later lessons talk about planning a budget. Farmers need to do all those things to be successful, don't you think?"

"Yes, indeed." Mother joined Allister at the table. "Studying this subject with Allister is one way we can help Father, Jim."

"Oh, alright!" Jim sat down beside Allister so he could see Allister's textbook too.

When they finished the first lesson and Jim left, Mother didn't budge. "How's it going, Allister?"

"I thought all the normal commotion in our one-room schoolhouse would distract me, but it hasn't. I'm able to concentrate, block out most of it. Miss Thompson laid out the work, gave me some instruction before the school day started, and left me on my own."

"You've always been good at working independently. You never really needed someone telling you what to do every minute." Mother smiled. "That has been true even with the work you've done on our farm. Allister, I'm proud of you. You are trying to do something that won't be easy. I believe you will succeed."

"Thanks, Mother."

"You're happy to be studying again, aren't you?"

"Absolutely. I finally have something in addition to my King James Bible to sink my mental teeth into, and it's already delicious!" Allister gave his mother a wide grin.

———◆———

At 8:30 the next morning, Allister found out his second attempt at the algebra was more successful. Miss Thompson gave him about ten minutes of instruction on the next algebra lesson, suggesting he read ahead each day to see if he could understand the next part on his own and be ready to ask her questions the next day.

Opening the French text and pulling out his homework, she quizzed him on the vocabulary, asking him to write the French on the board for English words she told him. Since the exercise appeared easy for him, she dictated sentences for him to translate into French. Then she quizzed Allister on the two short dialogues from the first two lessons without letting him look at the book. Finally she said, "You speak French, don't you? How did you learn it?"

"My family and I came from Quebec. I learned it from school-mates there."

"Then maybe you could pass the exam in this subject without studying it."

"Don't think I'd better do that. The textbook French is a little different from the conversational language I speak. But I should be able to go through this book fairly quickly. Did you take more than one year?"

"Yes."

"Then I'll try to finish both years' work by next March."

"One advantage of being an independent student, Allister, is that you can go at your own pace." Miss Thompson handed him the homework she'd marked and a list of additional assignments in each subject. "One more thing. At Cherry Creek, we read several classics besides our literature book. The first one I've selected for you is *David Copperfield* by Charles Dickens. I put it on your desk."

When Allister sat at his desk, he thought of the books his vicar friend, Reverend Wood, had lent him over the years. *Another one by Dickens. I can't wait to read it!* He had to force himself to set it aside to work on his other assignments.

———————

During recess later in the morning, Georgie interrupted Allister, begging him to come out to play with the boys of the school. "Alright, alright. I need a break anyway!"

"Yay!" Georgie yelled.

"Let's play tackle football," Johnnie said when Allister joined the boys outside.

Sides were chosen and the play began. Snap of the bladder "ball" was followed by yelling and throwing. A boy named Charlie caught the ball. Run, run, thump. Pop! Charlie's suspenders popped off. When he tried to stand up, his pants fell down. A collective howl of laughter erupted. Grabbing his pants, Charlie made for the sidelines, face red.

Allister had seen which direction the boy's buttons had flown. After a brief search, he picked them off the ground. "Here's your pants' buttons, Charlie."

The game continued. This time a tackler grabbed a handful of Johnnie's shirt, tearing it.

"Oh boy, is my mother going to be mad!" Johnnie tried to tuck the tatters back into the waist of his pants.

One more snap of the ball and tackle yielded the likelihood of another "pants down" incident. All of Allister's suspender buttons had been ripped off this time. Before he stood up, he knew he had to hold onto his pants. "That's enough!" Allister objected loudly. "Let's play soccer or something else."

"Sorry, Allister," Georgie said. "We'll find your buttons."

The boys in Georgie's grade scoured the playground until they retrieved all six buttons. By the time they did, recess was over. When Allister showed Miss Thompson the handful of buttons, she provided him with enough safety pins to hold up his pants until his mother could sew the popped buttons back on.

———◆———

Back at his desk, Allister turned his attention to his first composition. Using his memory of all the reading he had done so far, he was to write a two-page paper on a quote from Mr. Goggins, Superintendent of the North-West Territory Schools: "The purpose of education is to make a nation of worthy citizens."

When Allister thought about the topic sentence, he felt two pages was in no way long enough to talk about all the aspects of the subject. First there was the importance of having a common language. It's difficult to be a good citizen of a community if you can't talk to each other. He thought about his experiences in Lachute and with Stalking Deer, Sammy Le Feete, and the Dirksen family. Pioneer life on the prairies was difficult enough without having language and cultural differences to work through. Needing more time to organize his thoughts, he wrote some notes and set the assignment aside again.

Thinking there was time to begin the huge novel lying on his desk, he opened it and read a few lines. "Whether I shall turn out to be the hero of my own life, or whether that station will be held by anybody else, these pages must show …" Allister was hooked. During the walk home and back at dinner break, he continued to read. At one o'clock, he forced himself to set aside *David Copperfield* to do the assignments of other subjects.

Half an hour before the end of the school day, he returned to his literature book. There he was introduced to the words of William Wordsworth, in the poem "My Heart Leaps Up," for the very first time:

My heart leaps up when I behold
A rainbow in the sky;
So was it when my life began;
So is it now I am a man;
So be it when I shall grow old,
Or let me die!
The child is father of the man;
And I could wish my days to be
Bound each to each by natural piety.

Savoring the sounds, feelings, and wisdom in the poet's words, Allister walked home saying the poem over and over to himself.

———

Pouring himself into his first week of ninth-grade studies caused those five days to fly by. On Saturday during chores, Allister talked to John about the problem with the desk at school.

"Sorry, Allister. I don't really have time to make a bigger one for you, but I'll tell you how to make one for yourself during your school's Christmas vacation."

After breakfast, Allister spread out his homework on the dining room table. Father left his newspaper in the kitchen. Carrying his second cup of tea, he stood near Allister, looking over his shoulder. "You've been staring at those pages for hours. Bet you haven't made much progress," Father grumped.

Allister gulped. *Heavenly Father, please tell me how to respond.*

His father didn't move. He took another sip of tea. "I still think more study is a gigantic waste of your time."

Maybe he is just a little curious about what a ninth grader studies. Allister looked up at his father. "Yes, you were right to say that trying to do ninth grade would be difficult."

"Told you so, didn't I?" Father set his cup and saucer on the table.

When his father had joined him at the table, Allister continued. "My first week back at school had a rough start. On Monday, the teacher refused to even talk to me the whole day, but I wouldn't leave the school until she did. Since then, she's piled on the work. I'm studying so much because she seems to want to drown me. She even started me with the toughest subjects, botany and algebra!"

"Sounds like she wants you to give up! I know *I* would. ... But you aren't, are you?"

Allister squared his shoulders and shook his head.

Father reached for one of the books on the table. "What's this book about?"

"Agriculture, farming."

"And this book?"

"Botany, plants."

"Really? And this book?"

"Bookkeeping, the kind of math you use for business."

"But a farmer needs to know about all these things!"

"Yes, I know."

Father sat for a while, finishing his tea.

"Those aren't the only subjects I'm studying. There are a half dozen more."

Father didn't seem to hear him. Picking up the agriculture book, he leafed through a few pages until he found ones on grain farming. "Hmm ... here's something about a grain I don't know. Read it to me, son, if you don't mind."

When Allister finished the page, Father got up. "Thanks, son," he said. "You should teach Mother and Jim about the bookkeeping. I've always been a little short on the business end of farming."

"I already am."

A look of surprise flashed across his father's face and then he smiled at Allister for the first time in a long time. "Well, I'd better check at the elevators about that millet. Order some seed. Try it here."

Allister was elated. *I do believe Father finally understands that more education can really be useful, even for a farmer! I think now he's beginning to see it isn't a waste of my time!*

"Allister, there is something else you should consider. The teacher might have a reason for not wanting you in her school. Helping you with the ninth grade will make more work for her. As the teacher of all subjects for all the grades, she already has a full load."

"Guess it never occurred to me. You're right. Asking for her help with the ninth grade likely added a great deal to her workload," Allister said. "I *am* trying to help her. I'm going early to stoke and light the schoolhouse stove."

"Probably isn't enough. Think of something else you can do to help her if you're really determined to do the ninth grade."

"Alright, Father. I will."

chapter eleven

Teacher's Assistant

At dinner the same day, Mother told Allister she wanted him to go with her, Jessie, and Tawny to visit Sofi again. "You might need to split more firewood for the family," Mother reminded him.

After Allister had gotten Shalazar, the buggy, and the tools ready, he felt he should stick a hammer and a bag of nails in the back too.

When they pulled up to the scrubby oak in front of Sofi's Soddy, Allister saw a wagon full of lumber next to the open-sided shelter, and two horses tethered out to graze on the prairie grass. The smoke coming from the Soddy's stove pipe no longer smelled of dung. It was wood smoke.

Three little girls bounced out the door, with Lucy leading the way. A tall, bearded, blond-headed man followed them. "Hello. Sofi, see tell me you Annie," he said, handing Mother out of the buggy. "I Dietrich. Velcome our little haus."

Lucy pointed at Allister. "Papa, dat Alli-ser."

"Allister," Allister repeated, correcting her pronunciation.

"I meet you, Allister." Dietrich smiled and shook Allister's hand.

As soon as Allister lifted down Jessie and Tawny, Lucy and Hilda grabbed both of Jessie's hands. Greta stood behind them and put her arm around Tawny's neck.

Tawny licked Greta's cheek, and the little girl giggled.

Guess Greta is no longer afraid of Jessie's dog. Allister smiled. *That's good.*

"Come, come," Dietrich said to Mother and Allister.

Sofi was all smiles. Handing her baby to Mother, she bustled about the stove making coffee and cutting pieces of a sweet treat. "Streusel," Sofi said. "Berry come from montan."

"Raspberry," Mother said after her first bite. "Umm … very good! Thank you!"

After struggling through other bits of broken English, Mother changed the topic. "Allister, my boy here," she said, laying her hand on his arm, "went to school on Monday."

"School?" Dietrich sounded excited. "You have school?"

"Yes, we do." Allister lined up some kitchen items on the table. Pointing at an item one at a time, he demonstrated relative locations. "Our house, our barn, the school, my brother John's farm along the road."

"Mein haus … school … how far?"

Allister looked at Mother.

"About two miles," she said.

"Too far. Mein da-ter … little." Dietrich frowned. "See lost, yes?"

"I drive a school buggy," Allister offered, looking at Mother and shrugging his shoulders.

"School have buggy?" Dietrich asked.

Allister opened the door and pointed at Mother's buggy. "I can drive our buggy to school. It's alright, isn't it, Mother? I should've asked you before offering rides to school."

"That's a wonderful idea!" she agreed. Turning to Sofi, Mother asked, "How old is Lucy?"

Sofi shook her head and looked at her husband.

"See is seben. Hilda is sik," their father said. "Lucy go school sik months Ukraine. We teach her in haus German read."

"On Monday, I'll come here. With the buggy." Allister pointed at the buggy and the eight of the clock on the table. "At eight o'clock." He pointed at the two girls. "Pick up Lucy and Hilda. Take them to school with me in the buggy. Alright?"

After Dietrich and Sofi had talked a minute, he said, "Ya! Tank you."

"Dietrich, are you going to build a house?" Allister asked.

When the man didn't answer, Allister went outside to get the hammer and nails he happened to bring along. "Do you want me to help you?"

Dietrich's face broke into the biggest smile. "Ya, tank you."

The two worked the rest of the afternoon at the top of the ravine bank, constructing a frame for a house with its back to the turf roof of the Soddy.

"Cellar," Dietrich said, pointing at the sod house.

———◆———

Monday morning, Allister kept his promise to pick up and bring Lucy and Hilda to school. By the time Miss Thompson arrived, he had thought out what he would say to her about these new challenges to her teaching day.

After the teacher had taken off her coat and sat at her desk, Allister brought the two little girls to her. Pointing at the teacher, he said, "This is Miss Thompson. She is our teacher. Miss Thompson, this is Lucy. She is seven. This is Hilda. She is six. They are new neighbours from the Ukraine. They speak very little English. Lucy might know a few letters."

"Hello, Lucy. Hello, Hilda. It's nice to meet you."

Allister watched the teacher's face carefully. He could see she wasn't happy about having to teach two children English on top of everything else.

"Excuse me for a minute, Miss Thompson," he said. "I'll get one of the older girls to help with the orientation of our new students and then I'll come back in."

Taking Lucy and Hilda outside, he called Emily over and introduced the girls to her. "Emily, you remember what it was like on our first day at Wood Lake School five years ago, don't you? Well, this is Lucy and Hilda's first day at our school. They don't speak much English, but they need to know about the girls' outhouse and the pump. Would you help them?"

Emily smiled and grabbed their hands. "Come on, Lucy, Hilda, I'll show you."

When he came back to the teacher's desk, Allister said, "I'll help you with any group or grade you choose for an hour each day. Just tell me the time and the subject, or subjects."

"Thank you for your offer, Allister," she said. "Preparing your assignments and correcting your work is taking about an hour of my time after school. I'll think about your offer and let you know when it would help me the most."

While he went towards the schoolhouse door to join the children outside, Allister thought about the buggy rides with Lucy and Hilda to and from school. *Might as well use that time to help the girls learn more English. On the ride home this afternoon, I'll start by teaching them how to count and say six and seven correctly.* Allister smiled to himself. *A teacher's assistant. Didn't know I would be taking on such a job when I volunteered to give Lucy and Hilda rides to school.*

chapter twelve

Gaining Time

Early December, Allister and his twin brother, Jim, would be turning eighteen. Allister doubted this birthday would be special in any way. He and Jim were no longer little boys eagerly anticipating a party, a cake, and presents. To tell the truth, he'd seen little in the way of any family preparation, so he half expected their birthday to come and go without notice.

The evening of their birth date, however, Dan, Joe, and Mary showed up unexpectedly. Mother brought out a cake she had baked. John fetched a container he had hidden in the basement, and Father returned from a trip he'd made on Shalazar to another homestead.

One surprise was in John's container. He scooped out vanilla ice cream to go with Mother's yellow cake, all covered with chocolate icing. Allister savored the smooth feel of the frozen cream—his first taste of ice cream. Two other surprises were the birthday gifts.

"Sit down, Allister; close your eyes and hold out your hands," Mother said. "Don't peek. First, try to guess what it is." She placed a round, flat, metal object in his palm.

Smiling and scrunching his eyes closed, Allister ran his fingers over the gift's hard surface. A little larger than a quarter and fairly heavy for its size, it seemed to have designs in the metal, front and back. There was a knob on one side that turned and a hinged piece of metal that swivelled over and back above the knob. His fingertips discovered a second knob. When he pushed it in, one side of the metal object flew up to allow his fingers to touch a smooth glass surface. *Could it be my father's pocket watch? No, not a chance. Surely he won't give up his prize. Father would never part with anything so valuable.* Allister mumbled, "Not sure."

"Hold it up to your ear," Mother suggested.

Allister listened to its ticking. "A pocket watch."

Father laughed. "You may open your eyes now, son. Happy birthday! You'll make more use of it than I ever did."

Allister admired the intricate etchings on the metal case of the watch. He opened and closed the cover over its face. He looked with awe at its Roman numeral lettering and the delicate hour and minute hands. It was the watch his father had bought for himself at Desford's general store two years ago.

"Thank you so much, Pa!" The affectionate word for his father flew out of his mouth for the first time—unbidden. When he looked up to see how his father would respond, he was surprised to see his iron-willed, taciturn father blink. Had there been tears? Allister wasn't sure.

I've always known my mother loves me, Allister thought. *Maybe my father does, too, after all.* He secretly hoped his father's gift meant their relationship was finally warming up.

"Jim, your present is outside," John announced. "To keep it a surprise, we must tie a blindfold around your head."

John and Dan led Jim half way across the farmyard. Allister followed and saw Joe holding Shalazar. On his back was a saddle Allister had never seen before.

"Put your hands here, Jim," John and Dan directed. "What is it?"

Allister watched Jim run his hands over the smooth leather, feel its shape, and move the metal stirrup that hung down. "A saddle!" Excited, Jim ripped off his blindfold and touched the leather with obvious delight.

"Traded a calf for it," Father said. "Isn't new, but it's in good condition."

"Splendid!" Jim exclaimed. "Thanks so much, Father."

"You now have a saddle, but no horse," Dan teased. "Any idea how you will get one?"

"Easy!" Jim said. "I'll earn enough to buy one next fall—after I have worked on the local threshing crew."

Turning to Mother, he added, "In the meantime, you can use my saddle, if you will let me ride Shalazar sometimes."

"Of course, son," she said. "Happy birthday!"

Christmas and the lengthy school vacation that usually followed provided Allister with time he knew he couldn't waste. At his request, Miss Thompson had given him a mountain of assignments Allister planned to finish before school started again.

During the fall semester, he had taken the time to count the number of books Wood Lake School had acquired over the years he'd been a full-time farmer. More than three hundred now lined the book shelves of the one-room schoolhouse. He set his mind to read all of the ones he hadn't yet read ... before the end of June.

Two other jobs Allister wanted to complete before heading back to the schoolhouse included building himself a more comfortable desk and helping his mother and Jim set up a bookkeeping journal for the farm.

True to his promise, John helped Allister draw a design for a desk and chair. Using lumber from the stack near the machine shed, he followed John's instructions for measuring twice and cutting once. *Ah,* Allister thought as he tried out the new furniture he had built, *no more scrunching. No more cramped muscles. Finally, a desk as tall as I am.*

Allister's idea about using a bookkeeping journal to track farm income and expenses didn't work out as well. At his request, Mother managed to purchase the correct ledger for the bookkeeping. Allister was able to use what he had learned from his ninth-grade bookkeeping course to set up the appropriate columns for the family's homestead business. Entering all the right digits, however, proved to be a problem for Jim, much to Allister's surprise.

"Why are you having so much trouble with these columns of numbers?" Allister asked. "You were so good with arithmetic at school."

Jim stared at a page of the ledger in front of him and frowned. "Too tedious. Not as much fun as training a horse."

Allister grimaced and rolled his eyes. *Have to admit my brilliant idea isn't working. I assumed Jim would be excellent at bookkeeping. Seems he can't be bothered with the details. Apparently only Mother is patient enough to follow through with the required double entry system.*

Allister sighed. "Alright, Jim. I'll make sure Mother knows how to keep the books, and I'll check her work in the journal. But you'll still have to do your part."

"What's that?" Jim grumped.

"Remember to give her all the receipts and bills of sale for everything you buy or sell."

Jim groaned. "Thought being a farmer was a way of life. Guess I've never thought of farming as a business."

"Well, it is. I'm fairly sure that Pa thinks it is."

As Allister stuffed the ledger into a drawer in the dining room hutch, it dawned on him that view of farming might be the very reason his father's attitude had changed and he had become more supportive of Allister's efforts to finish his ninth-grade subjects. A couple of his subjects this year had been directly related to being a better farmer.

Ninth-grade studies had been about a great deal more than farming. Allister's mind raced while it ran in many directions. Independent student. Volunteer school buggy driver. Teacher's assistant. Monitor of the bookkeeping for his Pa's farm. And then there were the ninth-grade exams to prepare for. Passing those might mean he could go to high school. *How am I going to get everything done? The months are flying by. Lord, show me how to organize my time.*

chapter thirteen

Out of Time

With the arrival of calves, foals, chicks, and the slop, slop of Shalazar's hooves on wet road during his school buggy runs, Allister knew his study time was almost up. He'd studied very hard and hoped that when Pa insisted he stop, he could leave school with the confidence he had studied enough to pass the ninth-grade exams.

The Victoria Day holiday at the end of May came and so did his father's demand for Allister to return to the fields.

"Alright, Pa," Allister responded. "Just let me spend one more day at school. I want to say goodbye to Miss Thompson and the other students."

"Must you?" Father grumped.

"Yes, Pa. I owe her a big thank you for all her extra work on my behalf, at the very least. Don't you agree?"

The look of annoyance on his father's face vanished. "Of course, son. But I expect you full-time in the fields after that."

At the end of the school day the following Tuesday, Allister told Lucy and Hilda to wait for him outside for a few minutes.

After the girls left the building, he stopped by his teacher's desk. "Miss Thompson, I won't be coming to school for the next three weeks. Pa says I must help with the planting."

The teacher looked up from the scribblers she was correcting. "I'm sorry you have to leave so soon."

"I've cleared out my desk and will leave it here for now. One of the older boys is welcome to use it until the end of June. I'll pick it up later."

"Thank you, Allister. I remember you said you wanted to pass the ninth-grade exams. Are you still planning to take them at the end of June?"

"Yes, I am planning to take them."

"Are you ready?"

"Yes, I think so ... well, as ready as I could get after missing six weeks last fall and all of this last month of school. I probably need to review, but that will have to be done after each day's farm work is done and the sun has set."

"Alright, Allister. You'll need these, then." Miss Thompson handed him the pile of books he had been using. "Bring them back the day before you take the tests."

"Thank you, Miss Thompson. And thank you for all your help this year."

"You're welcome, Allister. You have been an excellent student. Although I had my misgivings at the beginning about your presence in my classroom, you have proved to be a definite asset. Thank you for all the help you gave me with the other students.

"The exam proctor at the high school knows me. I am sure I can get you into the test, but you'll have to go to Cherry Creek to take the exams. And you'll probably have to pay a fee for them, since your parents don't pay a property tax to the Cherry Creek School District."

"Alright, Miss Thompson. Just send Georgie over with a note about when the exams will be and how much their fee is."

On the teacher's desk, Allister placed a package wrapped in clean butcher paper and tied with a piece of colourful yarn. "Here's a small gift my mother made to give to you. Now if you'll excuse me, I need to get Lucy and Hilda home. You don't need to worry, Miss Thompson, about the girls getting to school from now on. Their father says he will make sure they get here. On the drive this morning, Lucy said something about her father trading a heifer for a pony. Hope those girls know how to ride."

Miss Thompson chuckled. "Well, if they don't, they'll soon learn."

Allister nodded and thought of all the times in the past when he had tussled with Shalazar. The rascal had gradually become a steady buggy horse and had faithfully brought Lucy, Hilda, and him to and from school this year without a fuss.

As he reluctantly left the schoolhouse, Allister sighed. *Farming takes priority over my education once again.* Purposefully thrusting aside his anxiety over his upcoming solo push through exam preparation, Allister smiled. *That lacy, white collar Mother made for Miss Thompson is beautiful. I am sure she'll like it.*

chapter fourteen

Tests and the Dodge

Running his hands nervously along the worn cloth strap of his school bag, Allister stood in front of Cherry Creek's stone schoolhouse. It didn't look as imposing as he remembered it, but then he had been a good deal younger the last time he'd seen it.

Opening the massive wooden door, he walked down the hallway. His footsteps echoed against the glass windows in the classroom and office doors and off the plastered walls. When he tried the classroom door where he'd been told the exams would be held, it was locked.

Allister checked the time on Pa's pocket watch. He was early. Mother had lent him Shalazar, and Jim had loaned him his saddle, to make sure Allister would be on time. She'd even given him money to board the horse for the day at the livery stable.

Fifteen minutes before the start of the exams, the proctor and a teacher arrived. With the arrival of more students, registration began. Allister proudly paid his fee out of his own savings from the threshing crew work he'd done. When all of the test takers were seated, he took out his writing supplies and put his book bag and dinner pail along the wall in front of the room with the other students' things. Several of the students stared at him. *They probably all know each other,* he thought. *They're wondering who I am.*

Back at his seat, Allister set Pa's pocket watch in front of him on the desk. Rubbing his sweaty palms on his pants' legs, he took a deep breath.

Letting it out slowly, he prayed silently, *Lord, order my thoughts and help me to recall all I have studied.*

The proctor wrote two instructions in giant letters on the front board: NO CHEATING. NO TALKING. He also gave specific directions about how to ask him for help if a student didn't understand how to do a section of the test. "We'll take a short break at the end of each exam. The first one is on reading and language. You'll have two hours. You may start … now!"

Remembering what the eighth-grade exam proctor had said about test taking, Allister looked through the whole test. Identifying the part that would take the most time, he raced through the others. Then he took his time with the difficult section. When he'd finished, he flipped open the watch. Twenty more minutes. It was enough time to check his work.

Closing his exam book and returning the watch to his pocket, Allister turned in the exam book and his test scribbler a few minutes early. Surprise registered on the proctor's and a few of the students' faces.

Remembering the proctor said there was to be a break at the end of each exam section, Allister left the building to use the outhouse. He ambled around to the front of the school to find its pump and get a drink.

Back in the exam room, it was time for the algebra test. Allister was more anxious about this section. But he soon found that while he was no genius at math, his thoroughness and methodical approach to problem solving helped him complete it in time.

At dinner break, most of the students walked home. Allister joined a few of the young people on the nearby grass. Eating his meatloaf sandwich and raspberry jam tarts in silence, he listened while the others talked. From what they said, Allister guessed they lived on farms within a few miles of town. The fact that no one had made any effort to include him in their conversation made Allister uneasy. *Should I introduce myself?* He pondered. *If I do, what name do I give? Don't want any more teasing about the name Allister.*

"Hello, my name's William Taylor, and he's Russell McKinnon," one teenager said, finally including Allister.

"I'm glad to meet you. I'm … Robert McRuer." Allister gave his first, rather than his middle, name. Hoping he had successfully dodged being teased about his name, he added, "You can call me Bob." Allister smiled and thought about the day on the Pembina River when Jim had called him "Bob the log."

Allister studied the younger teen, Russell. *Is he the son of Peter McKinnon, the driver Jim and I helped our first day in Cherry Creek seven years ago?*

"You didn't attend Cherry Creek this year." William brought Allister back to the moment.

"No, I was an independent student at a rural school," Allister said.

"Well, good luck! Hope you pass, McRuer!" Russell added.

"Thank you! Hope you do too."

———————

The exams took two days. Not everyone took the last two parts, agriculture and French, so only a few students were left in the exam room when Allister turned in the test for the first year of French and asked for the second-year form.

After he had turned in the last exam book, he asked, "How will you let me know my marks?"

"We usually post the results on the school's bulletin board in the hallway," the proctor said.

"Sir, I live near Desford, twelve miles away. Could you mail me my marks?"

"No. Sorry, son. We've never had a rural student take these exams before. You'll have to come in to see your marks."

"When?"

"Should be posted by one o'clock one week from today."

"Alright. Thank you for letting me sit for the exams."

———————

Relieved the exams were over, Allister went to the livery stable to fetch and saddle Shalazar. On the ride home, Allister's mind meandered through the questions and answers on the tests. *Have I done well enough to pass?* His stomach was in knots by the time he got home.

"The proctor said a week," Allister muttered as he turned Shalazar into the pasture with the other horses. "How will I ever endure the week?"

Later that day, his father's query didn't help any. "Mother said you finished the ninth- grade exams. Think you'll pass?"

chapter fifteen

The Proof

A week later, Allister begged both Mother and Jim to come with him to Cherry Creek. At one o'clock, the school's foyer was crowded with high school students and their parents. The proctor pinned up the tenth-grade marks first.

Allister felt for all the world like their Guernsey cow, Bessie, must have felt when she was trying to deliver her over-sized, breech birth calf. *What agony! I am so glad Mother and Jim agreed to accompany me today.*

At last the proctor pinned up the ninth-grade results, test by test. Gradually the crowd thinned.

"Hey, McRuer, congratulations! You aced everything, including second year French! Look!" Russell stood next to a list, pointing.

"Thank you," Allister said. "How did you do?"

"Passed everything. That's what's important, I guess."

"Going to attend Cherry Creek High School next fall?"

"You bet. See you then?"

"Maybe."

"Alright, bye."

Taking out a slip of paper, Allister wrote down his exam marks for each subject. When he was finished, he asked Mother to verify that he had written them correctly and gave her the paper.

She put the list in her pocket and promised to show Pa. "I'm so proud of you, son!" she said, hugging him.

"Way to go, brother o'mine!" Jim exclaimed, slapping Allister on the back.

———◆———

In the evening after supper, Mother handed Pa the list of exam marks while Allister was still sitting at the kitchen table. Pa studied the scores with puckered brow and let out a low whistle.

"Pa?" Allister was finally able to make his tongue say something, although it felt as stiff as a kiln-dried brick.

"Yes, son?"

"You know what this means, don't you?"

When his father didn't answer, Allister added, "I'm qualified in every way to attend Cherry Creek High School next September!"

Before heading out the back door to do chores, Allister glanced at his father. Pa was still sitting at the kitchen table with his brows knit tight, a frown on his face, and his arms folded across his chest.

Pa has no real reason to stop me now. Thank you, Lord God.

I am no longer fourteen. In a few months, I will be nineteen. And I have proved I can pass high school subjects. Allister's smile grew. *Will Pa let me leave home and the farm to go to high school? I don't know.*

chapter sixteen

Face-off

Allister's memory of his father's frown and silence about his desire to leave the farm bothered him all summer. He still didn't know if his father would let him go when it was time to start school in the fall.

Reinforcements are what I need. People who will support me. But who? Mother? Mary? Joe? I counted on their support years ago. None gave it. What advice did Mary give me then? Wait. Try later. Well, I waited. I tried later like she advised. Who then? John? Allister remembered that John had helped Will negotiate his departure for his own homestead. *John even defended Will's right to build his homestead the way he wished. Pa backed down. Maybe John would support me.*

During the very next work session on John's homestead claim, Allister showed his oldest brother his ninth-grade exam marks. While he helped John fork stacks of hay, Allister revisited a conversation they'd had some time ago. "I don't know if you remember, but I told you once I didn't want to farm. I also told you I wanted to go to high school so I would have a better foundation for building my future."

John stopped forking the hay and stared at Allister. "Yes, I remember. So that's what completing your ninth-grade studies was all about? You were getting yourself ready for high school?"

Allister nodded.

"Well, you did well enough on those exams to prove to yourself and everyone else that you can certainly handle high school."

"Registration for classes is at the end of August," Allister said. "I'll need your help to make sure I can get there."

"My help?"

"Yes. When I ask Pa for permission to leave the farm so I can live in Cherry Creek and attend school, I could use some support. He is sure to object because I'll have to leave before the harvest is in."

"Hmm. You're right." John stuck his fork into some hay. "Tell me when you want me there. I'll give you my support. You have certainly earned this chance."

"Thanks, John."

———————

Dan's request for help in digging a well on his homestead claim gave Allister plenty of time to ask him for support as well. Remembering Dan's enthusiastic remarks about farming caused Allister to hesitate to ask. But Allister remembered Dan had also said to give farming a try. *Well, I have—for four years.*

Allister steeled himself and asked. Although Dan tried, at first, to talk Allister out of pursuing his dream, in the end he promised to come when Allister planned to talk to their father about leaving.

Jim, however, was the one person Allister knew would be no help whatsoever. When he tried to talk to his twin about leaving to continue his schooling, Jim just said, "I already told you Father wouldn't let you. Why do you still want to leave? Why dream about doing something you can't do? Yes, high school is no longer as far away as Brandon. It's now available in Cherry Creek. But that doesn't matter one bit. You know Father hasn't changed his mind. Besides, you are the only one in the family with a ninth-grade education. More than any of the rest of us have. You have nothing to complain about."

After Jim stomped off, Allister wondered about the real reason behind Jim's obstinate refusal to be the usual supportive brother. *For eighteen years, we have spent almost every moment together. Is he worried about having to do things by himself, worried about being lonely? Or could it be he doesn't want to be the only son left on the family farm? Is he afraid he'll get stuck with all of the chores?*

The weeks of July and most of August sped by. Allister knew he would need to register for classes at Cherry Creek High School the very next week if he was going to attend that fall. The thought of confronting his father one more time tied his stomach in knots, but he couldn't wait any longer.

After asking Mother if Dan could join them for dinner after church the next Sunday, Allister trotted the mile over to Dan's homestead with the invitation. Getting that brother's agreement to be there, Allister also told John of his plans to make his request after dinner on Sunday. John assured Allister he would stay after the meal to lend his support.

During Sunday dinner, Mother's delicious roasted chicken and potato salad seemed to stick in Allister's craw. *Do I dare challenge Father in this way? It will mean I won't be here to help with harvest this year. But how else can I build my own future?*

As soon as the meal was ended, Allister cleared his throat. "Pa, it is time."

"Time for what, Allister?" Father put down his tea cup.

"For me to register for my high school classes."

"What?"

"I passed all my ninth-grade exams. Remember?"

When his father didn't respond, Allister rattled on. "I'm qualified to continue my education. In a few months, I will be nineteen. Old enough to move into town. All I need is your permission."

Allister held his breath and looked from John to Dan. Out of the corner of his eye, Allister saw Jim slump at the table and Jessie's face reflect surprise.

"Old enough now? Yes." Father growled. "Had some ninth-grade subjects that were helpful for farming? Yes. But I haven't changed my mind. I still believe no farmer needs a high school diploma!"

"Let Allister go to high school, Father," John said. "He is a capable student. A good education always helps a person build a better future."

Allister saw his father's jaw tighten. "What about this year's harvest? I need every hand available."

"Don't worry about it," John said. "I'm here. I can help you. So can Dan. Right, Dan?"

Dan nodded. "Joe usually works with us too. Even without Allister, you'll have plenty of threshing crew, any way you look at it. Let him go."

Allister looked at his mother. She was smiling.

"Yes, Father. Allister is right. It is time for him to go."

"Well, I object," Jim growled. "If Allister leaves, I'll have to do all the chores by myself."

Allister glanced at Jim. *Ah ha! I thought so.*

"All the chores? You?" Jessie spouted. "What about me? I'm eleven." She puffed out her chest. "I do chores too. You forget, Jim?"

Jim groaned. "Jessie, I didn't mean ... Sorry, Jessie. You do chores and do a good job too." He rested his elbows on the table and put his chin in his hands.

Silence settled over the kitchen. No one stirred for several minutes.

Father sighed and stood up. "Alright, son. If this is what you are sure you want to do, you can go. But if you do, I can't help you. You will be on your own."

Allister jumped up and hugged his father. "Thanks, Pa."

His father grabbed Allister and held him at arm's length. Gazing up into Allister's face, he asked, "When do you leave?"

"Tomorrow. I need to go into town to register."

"Then you'll need to find a place to stay and a job to support yourself. Remember I said you will be on your own."

As Allister turned to thank John and Dan for their support, the reality of the change in his situation sunk in for the first time. *Studying I know. Living on my own? How do I manage that?*

chapter seventeen

Becoming Bob

Allister stood for a long time staring at a sign in the corner of the drugstore's window. In bold letters, the sign read HELP WANTED. He had come into Cherry Creek to register for the tenth grade. But he had neither a place to live nor a place to work. He needed both.

Mother and he had prayed together before he rode to town, asking his Heavenly Father to provide a place to live and to give him a job to pay expenses. And now Allister was about to apply for his first job.

After tucking in his shirt and checking his hair in the mirror-like window of the storefront, he opened the door. A bell tinkled above his head. The man behind the counter looked up. Allister recognized him. It was Mr. Wright, the one who had helped "doctor" the injured driver on Allister and Jim's first day in Cherry Creek! But would the pharmacist recognize or remember even seeing Allister? It'd been seven years since he'd been in the store. He was a boy then. Now at six feet in height and a few months short of nineteen, he was a man.

"Hello, young man," Mr. Wright said, showing no sign of recognition. "What can I do for you?"

"You have a help wanted sign in the window."

"That's right. I need a part-time assistant."

"Well, sir, I'd like to apply. My name is Robert McRuer. I'm eighteen years old. I have a ninth-grade education. I've just registered for the tenth grade at the high school."

"Where are you from?"

"A farm at the foot of Turtle Mountain several miles east of Desford."

"So the only work you've done is farming?"

"No, sir. I've helped my father and brothers dig wells, build houses and barns, build the one-room school on our property, and make and lay brick for a house. I have also tutored children in math, reading, and English, and taught my mother and twin brother the bookkeeping I learned last year."

"Where did you learn bookkeeping?"

"At Wood Lake School. The new teacher, Miss Thompson, tutored me in ninth-grade subjects last year."

"Ah, Miss Thompson. She graduated from Cherry Creek."

"I know, sir. That's why I asked her to help me."

Mr. Wright stood, stroking and twirling an end of his thick, brown mustache.

"Is Wood Lake School where you tutored the children?"

"Yes, sir."

"Did you take the exams for the ninth grade?"

"Yes, sir. At Cherry Creek High School, here in town."

"When?"

"In June."

"This year?"

"Yes, sir."

"Did you pass all subjects?"

"Yes, sir, all subjects."

"Do you know anyone in town who could vouch for you?"

"Yes, sir. Reverend Wood, the vicar of St. Matthew's Anglican Church, and one other person."

"How do you know Reverend Wood?"

"When we first came to Manitoba, I borrowed books from him almost every time my family came to town. The Reverend was very kind to me. He was a good listener and gave me lots of good advice."

Mr. Wright smiled. "You said there was one other person in town who could vouch for you. Who is that person?"

"You, sir."

"Me?"

"Yes, sir. Seven years ago, my twin brother, Jim, and I stopped an injured driver from bleeding to death. His name was Peter McKinnon."

Mr. Wright's mouth dropped open. With a laugh, he said, "You'll have to forgive me for not recognizing you. You are a tad bit taller than you were seven years ago."

Allister grinned. "I know, sir."

"Alright, Robert McRuer. One part of the job in this drugstore is serving as the soda jerk after school and Saturday mornings. Do you think you could do that—run the soda fountain?"

"Yes, sir, I'm sure I can. I'm a quick learner."

"Then you're hired. I'll pay you ten cents an hour. There will be some work to do before you start school every day, several hours after school, and a half day on Saturday. My drugstore isn't open on Sunday. Can you start September 1?"

"Yes, sir. Thank you, Mr. Wright. This is wonderful!" Both astonished and excited, Allister thought, *So quickly. A job! Thank you, Lord! But where am I going to live? Help me find a place to stay.* Allister turned to go. "See you September 1."

"Wait a minute," the pharmacist called as Allister put his hand on the front door knob. "Do you have a place to stay?"

"No, sir, not yet."

"I have a room upstairs. In fact, I used to live up there. Would you like to see it?"

Allister could hardly believe his ears. "Yes, thank you, sir. I would."

The pharmacist locked the door of his store, turned a sign on it that read "Return in ten minutes," and led the way across the store to a back staircase. At the top of the stairs was a wide area that was obviously being used for storage. Across the middle of the wooden floor was a wall that rose about eight feet, leaving a gap between it and the tall ceiling of the second floor.

Mr. Wright took a ring of keys out of his storekeeper's apron pocket. In the semidarkness, he selected a key and unlocked the door in the middle of the wall.

Behind it was a room that took up the full width of the building. In the wall opposite the door, two sets of double windows looked out over the main street of the town. Scattered about the room were a wooden coat rack, parts of a single iron bedstead, a thin mattress rolled up, a small table, and two chairs. A narrow table along one wall had a metal cabinet on it. A tall, narrow cupboard, a washstand with a mirror, and a commode with a chamber pot completed the collection.

"If you would be willing to keep the furnace stoked," Mr. Wright added, "sweep the store's floors every day, and shovel snow away from the front and back doors, you could live here rent free."

Allister's mouth dropped open. *Living and working in the same place? Only two blocks from school? Couldn't be better!*

"Wonderful!" Allister exclaimed. "I'll be happy to do anything you ask."

"I didn't know where else to put my old furniture, so I just left it here," Mr. Wright explained. "You're welcome to use it or bring some things from home."

"Thank you," Allister said. "I don't have much to bring." Standing next to the narrow table, he lay his hand on the metal cabinet. *How odd!* It was two feet long and a foot high. "Excuse me, Mr. Wright, but what is this?"

"An oil stove. It works a little like a kerosene lamp, but without wicks. You'll have to buy coal oil for it. I'll show you how to operate it when you come back on August 31. You'll want to get settled in before you start work the next day."

"Thank you so much, Mr. Wright," Allister said. "I'll do my best to be a good worker and roomer—as well as a student."

"I'm sure you will. I lock up the drugstore at 6:00 p.m. Be sure to be here and moved in before that time on Thursday."

———————

"How did it go?" Pa asked when Allister came into the house after tending to Shalazar's needs.

"Unbelievably well," Allister exclaimed, grinning at Mother. "I'm registered for tenth-grade classes. I have a part-time job at the drugstore before and after school during the week and half day on Saturday. The pharmacist has invited me to stay in the room above the store where I'll be working. I'm to move into Wright's Drugstore Thursday afternoon and start work Friday morning."

His father stared at him, disbelief written all over his face.

"Guess I shouldn't be surprised you were able to complete everything in town and still be home in time for dinner," Mother said. "God answered every last one of our prayers very quickly. Timing must definitely be His!"

"Yes, indeed!" Allister agreed, handing her back the money she'd given him to board Shalazar for the day. "On top of that, the man at the livery stable wouldn't take a full day's board for the short time your horse was there."

Allister was so excited, he could hardly contain himself. What he had longed for during the last four years was finally happening. "Pa, I have two days to help with the fields. I can wait until Thursday morning to pack up since I don't have much to take with me."

In the evening, Mother quizzed Allister about what exactly was available to him in the room above the drugstore. During the next two days, while Allister drove the binder or stooked sheaves of oats with Pa, John, and Jim, she packed up everything she thought Allister might need. The morning of his departure she baked extra loaves of bread, an additional dozen biscuits, scones, and raspberry tarts.

Allister only needed to pack his wood crate with clothes and the two books he owned, the novel *Kidnapped* and his Bible. He remembered to grab his winter coat when he went out the back door.

John had agreed to drive Allister in a wagon to Cherry Creek and help him move into his new home. While John loaded all the crates Mother had packed for Allister, he hugged Jessie goodbye and stroked Tawny's head.

Wrapping his arms around his twin, Allister whispered in Jim's ear, "I'll likely miss you the most. Don't worry. I'll be back some Sundays whenever I can, and holidays too."

"Allister, where are you going?" Jessie asked.

"The big stone school in Cherry Creek. Remember? We went to visit Father there and we had a picnic."

"Oh yes, big school. Father built it when he was gone a long time."

"That's right."

Allister hugged his mother. "Pray for me," he whispered. Then louder, "Thanks for all the supplies."

Last of all, he shook hands with his father. "Thank you, Pa. I'll study and work hard." *Someday I hope you'll be proud of me,* he thought.

Hopping onto the wagon, John and Allister drove down their farm lane. Just as they turned west onto the main road, Dan ran up. "Had to say goodbye and good luck."

"Thanks, Dan. If you're ever in town, stop by Wright's Drugstore. That's where I'll be working and living when I'm not at school."

On the way to Cherry Creek, John stopped at Wood Lake School to pick up Allister's desk and chair. It was the only furniture they were bringing along.

———◆———

After they arrived at the drugstore and Allister had introduced Mr. Wright to John, the pharmacist asked John to drive around behind the store to unload everything. "Look, Allister," John said, "even in town there are outhouses. Can you believe the one down the block?"

Allister took a second look. It was a two-storey with a bridge between the upper part of the outhouse and the second floor of the building in front of it. He laughed. "Looks like those people don't have to climb down and upstairs to use it! I have no such luck."

After all of Allister's things were in his room, John helped him assemble the bed and move the furniture.

"Allister, you've waited years for this opportunity. Make the most of it!" John said as he stood at the back door to the store. "It won't come around twice."

"You know I will," Allister said, shaking John's hand. "Thanks for supporting my venture."

"You're welcome, Allister."

After John left, Mr. Wright led Allister to a corner at the back of the store. Opening a small door close to the floor, the pharmacist said, "This is our cooler. Its metal box sticks outside the back wall of the store. It keeps items cold from October through May. You're welcome to keep eggs, milk, butter, and other items in it whenever there's space."

Then he walked upstairs with Allister to show him how to operate the cabinet coal oil stove. "You told me your name's Robert, yet I heard John call you Allister."

"My given first name is Robert. Allister is my middle name. For some strange reason, Pa calls a couple of us by our middle names."

"What do you want to be called?"

"Robert or Bob."

"Bob it is, then! How many siblings do you have?"

"Six."

"How many of you does your father call by your middle names?"

"Two. John is the other one. Pa calls him Angus."

"Angus? That's odd!"

"Actually, it's fitting for him. Both Pa and John raise Angus cattle."

"Well, looks like you're almost settled in and your mother's looked after you well," Mr. Wright said, pointing at all the crates of supplies.

"Yes, sir, she's as delighted as I am that I finally get to go to high school."

"One more thing. It'd be best if you would separate your garbage into two tin buckets. You are welcome to use a couple of the buckets in the storage area. Have one for paper trash only. We burn that in the barrel next to our outhouse. The other is for any vegetable or fruit peelings. I'll take that home and put it on my wife's waste pile. She uses it to fertilize her garden in the spring.

"Here's a key for the back door in case you want to leave the building after hours. Please be careful to lock up, even if you only leave to use the outhouse. I'm trusting you to keep my store secure."

"Yes, sir. Thank you, Mr. Wright. I know I have a big responsibility."

The pharmacist smiled. "See you at eight tomorrow morning. Good evening, Bob."

"Good evening."

———

Alone at last, Allister sat on the bare mattress of his bed for a few moments. He marvelled at the silence. No busy household to flow around him. Even the street below the windows of his room was quiet. It was after business hours. Stores had evidently been locked up. Everyone must have gone home.

"Well, Mother's crates won't unpack themselves," Allister muttered. "Time to put my new home in order."

There were sheets, blankets, a pillow, and an old quilt in a couple of crates. From a third crate, he pulled out a windup alarm clock, towels, soap, cooking and eating equipment. In a fourth, Allister found matches, wicks, a bottle of kerosene, the lamp from his family's dining room table, and a container of coal oil for the cook stove. From two other crates, Allister took food supplies he knew had come from his mother's cellar and the family's farmyard. Smiling at the bounty his mother had given him, Allister found a place for everything. Stacking the empty packing crates sideways under one set of windows, he now had his own hopeful bookcase—hopeful because he was hoping to soon have more books.

After a supper of a reheated canning jar of Mother's chicken and dumplings soup, bread, raspberry tarts, and tea, the only remaining chore was washing his dishes. Finding the store's hand pump on the first floor, he filled a pot with water. Heating it on the stove, he did his dishes and carried the waste water downstairs to the outhouse.

It looks like a fine evening for a walk, he thought as he locked the empty pot inside the back door of the store. *I've never had much time to just wander the town.*

While he ambled along the town's streets, his mind raced in many directions. *How will I manage both school and work? The courses I will be taking look like they'll require tons of homework. Plus I have no idea how to run a soda fountain or a cash register. Will I be able to do everything Mr. Wright asks me to do?*

Back in his room before nightfall, Allister tried to settle in for the night. Everything felt strange. He was used to sleeping in a double bed with his twin brother. Here his bed was narrow. Every night at home, there had been Jim's slumbered breathing next to him and their father's snoring from the next room. Missing the usual sounds of his family members sleeping around him, Allister lay there, thinking about home.

Unable to sleep, he got up, sat at his desk, and lit the kerosene lamp. *I need to calm my spirit. Why is being alone adding to my anxiety?* Opening his Bible, Allister read several Psalms until he read a verse in chapter three. *"I laid me down and slept; I awaked; for the Lord sustained me."*[13]

Reassured, Allister blew out the lamp, crawled into bed, and slept.

———

Up at dawn without rooster crow, Allister opened a window and listened. Nothing was stirring, except a few birds. Since there were no animal care chores to do, he could take his time with his morning preparations. Dressed, he went downstairs with his chamber pot and teakettle to empty one and fill the other. Minus older brothers and a mother for the first time in his life, breakfast was a bit of a disaster. *Burnt or not, a McRuer doesn't waste food. I guess it's going to take me a while to learn how to manage these burners.*

Sitting at the table with a second cup of tea, he listened to Cherry Creek gradually come to life. First a few, then more and more people, horses, wagons, and buggies moved up and down the street.

Opening his Bible, Allister did his usual morning reading. In the day's chapter, he read and reread, *"… we glory in tribulations also: knowing that tribulation worketh patience; and patience, experience; and experience, hope; and hope maketh not ashamed; because the love of God is shed abroad in our hearts by the Holy Ghost which is given unto us."*[14] He thought, *These words sound so much like what God has been working out in my life these past four years.*

A few minutes before eight, he went downstairs. Mr. Wright was already at work. "Good morning, Bob," he said. "Your assistant's uniform is ready."

The pharmacist held out a white, bibbed, store apron and a pair of blue cloth covers to wear over the bottom half of Bob's shirt sleeves.

Hmm, that's right. I must think of myself as Bob if that's what I want everyone to call me, he thought. *I'm no longer Allister. After all, I have to keep in mind Bob is the name I have already given several schoolmates. Today I have a different kind of rebirth, a new identity. Well, Bob, what kind of man will you show yourself to be?*

chapter eighteen

Soda Jerk

"In colder weather," Mr. Wright said, "your first task will be to stoke the furnace in the basement with coal. Keep in mind, you might have to stoke the furnace more than once a day, during your dinner break at noon and again after I close the store at 6:00 p.m. But today, I'd like you to start with sweeping the floor."

After Bob put on his store assistant uniform, he swept along the wooden planks, studying the contents of each shelf and display case. *Sweeping a floor beats forking piles of dung any day. I wonder how messy shovelling coal into a furnace will be.*

Since the soda fountain with its curved counter and numerous stools was an addition to the drugstore he hadn't seen before, Bob tried unsuccessfully to figure out the use of the items he saw behind its glossy top. *Hmm. Another cabinet coal oil stove. Why use one of those at a soda fountain?*

When Bob finished the floor of the whole store, his boss handed him a feather duster, a pile of old newspapers, and a jar of vinegar. "Dust all surfaces and polish the glass of the display cases and front windows—inside and out," his boss said. "You'll find a ladder in the storage shed against the back of the store."

As Bob dusted, he watched Mr. Wright mix a combination of liquids in a gallon jar. Bob's curiosity was satisfied shortly after the store opened for business. While the pharmacist waited on customers out front, Bob was assigned to work in a cramped back office. His task was to fill and label freshly-washed glass bottles with the red liquid from the gallon jar. Catching a drop of it on his finger, he tasted cherry.

While he worked, he studied the bulky black machine that took up a lot of space on his boss's roll top desk. Sticking his head out the door of the office to make sure Mr. Wright wasn't busy with a customer, Bob called, "Mr. Wright, got a minute? I'd like to ask you a question." When the pharmacist came to the office door, Bob pointed at the black monstrosity on the roll top desk. "What is that?"

Mr. Wright laughed. "Never seen one before? It's a typewriter. Used it to make the labels you're pasting on those bottles. Whenever you have time in the evenings, you'll need to teach yourself to type. I'll be expecting you to make the labels yourself soon."

"Alright," Bob said, "but I'd like to watch you type for a few minutes first. I have no idea how it's done."

In spite of his fascination with all the new tasks he was attempting, Bob thought, *I already told my boss I'm quick. Got a lot to learn. Hope I can meet his expectations.*

When Bob thought he had two dozen bottles ready, he brought them out to the counter. Mr. Wright took one look at them and said, "Bob, you had better take these two back and redo their labels."

Bob gulped. *What could be wrong?*

Hurrying back to the office with the mislabelled bottles, Bob set them down and looked. *Oh, brother. How did that happen?* The labels were upside down. *I must have been studying the typewriter while I was pasting these. Better pay attention. Such a stupid mistake. What will Mr. Wright think of me?*

After repasting a couple of leftover labels on the bottles, Bob brought them out.

Mr. Wright smiled. "That's better. Now I want you to put all but three of the cough syrup on the second shelf behind the counter."

Setting out several items next to the three bottles, the pharmacist gave his new assistant a lesson in designing a front window display of merchandise. "Put samples of items in the display you are wanting or needing to sell," Mr. Wright said. "Sometimes they'll be goods that have just arrived or haven't sold; other times, you'll include seasonal things."

"Like the cough syrup you just mixed up?"

"Uh huh. The temperature change every fall seems to bring on the coughs and colds."

By noon, Bob had set up the displays in both front windows. *I wonder what Jim did this morning. Bet it wasn't as interesting as what I did.*

He went outside to see how the displays looked from the street. When he came back in, he rearranged a few things.

"Bob, it's dinner time. Come back in half an hour to give me a break so I can eat mine."

After running up the stairs to his room, Bob reheated the contents of a jar of his mother's beef stew and boiled water to make tea. This time, nothing burned or boiled over. Bob looked at the mess from breakfast. He thought about the spotless kitchen at home. *No mother to clean this up. Guess it's up to me.* Bob glanced at the clock on his desk. *No time now.*

Back behind the counter at 12:30, Bob waited on customers while Mr. Wright ate a cold sandwich in the back room. Whenever the customer was ready, the pharmacist came out to ring up the sale on the register and make change from the cash drawer. Bob thought, *I hope Mr. Wright will teach me how to manage the cash register soon.*

During the mid-afternoon lull, Mr. Wright had Bob practice ringing up a sale. It meant doing the mental arithmetic of adding up various items for a sale. While Bob practiced counting back change from different amounts paid, he couldn't help thinking about Jim. *He wouldn't have any trouble doing this. Me? Oh, boy!*

"Bob, if you really need to, pencil the amounts on this scrap piece of packaging paper by the cash register, but I'd rather you do it in your head."

Bob grimaced. *Thought I'd left the need for mental math behind.*

"Always take your time," Mr. Wright continued. "It's very important to be 100 per cent accurate. One mistake, and I lose customers."

Bob gulped. *That's what I am afraid of.*

About four o'clock, several teenagers came in and sauntered over to the soda fountain. Bob sized them up. *Look like they're high school students. A couple of years younger than me. Town kids. Bet they don't know the difference between a pitch fork and a stook.*

"Come watch, Bob." The pharmacist walked behind the counter. "What'll you have?" he asked the young people.

"Three root beers, please."

"Coming right up."

From the spigot of a quart jug sitting on a shelf along the brick wall opposite the soda fountain, Mr. Wright gave each of three tall glasses two squirts of root beer syrup. Turning around, he reached for the handles of the fountain heads next to the counter. Jerking them down, he filled each glass with phosphate. Sticking paper straws in the glasses, he gave each a quick stir before placing them in front of the teens. "Nine cents, please," the pharmacist said.

Ringing up the sale on a smaller cash register that sat on the table next to shelves, he said, "Bob, take their money and give them their change."

When Bob did, one of the boys said, "Hey, soda jerk, you new here? Where'd you come from? A farm?"

The other teens laughed.

Bob felt heat rise up his neck and flood his face. Feeling shame for growing up on a farm was a new experience for him. *These boys think they're better than me. They assume someone from a farm has no brains. Won't they be surprised when I sit in classes with them!*

Deciding to ignore the teen's taunt, Bob turned his attention towards a mother and her small son who came over to the counter to ask for two sodas—one cherry, one lemon. This time, Bob made the drinks and completed the sale.

About 5:30, Mr. Wright put a CLOSED sign on the soda fountain counter. "Time to clean up, Bob. After you wash the glasses, rinse them in a pan of scalding hot water. Be sure to use wooden tongs to lift the glasses out and set them upside down on a clean towel. Let them air dry."

Now Bob understood why there was a cabinet coal oil stove with two burners and two metal dish pans on a small table under the counter.

"When you've cleaned up, push this button on the register to open it, remove the cash drawer, and bring it to me in the back room. I lock the money up in the store safe every night until I have an opportunity to make a deposit in the bank. The best idea for you, Bob, since you live here, is to never tell anyone what I do with the store's money. Agreed?"

"Yes, sir." Bob gulped. *This great opportunity to work in and live above a main business in town comes with some big responsibilities. Father God*, he prayed silently, *help me to remain worthy of this man's trust.*

Bob set to work washing and rinsing the soda glasses. Momentarily distracted by his mental replay of the scene with the teens, their taunt and laughter, Bob reached for a glass in the scalding rinse water—without the tongs. "Ow!" The dropped glass shattered on the floor. *Oh no!*

From across the store, he heard Mr. Wright call to him. "Bob, are you alright? What happened?"

"Sorry, sir. Forgot to use the tongs. Dropped and broke a glass. I'll pay for it. You can take it out of my wages, sir."

"Don't worry, Bob. I'll forgive one broken glass. Just don't break another."

"Yes, sir." Bob stuck his burnt fingers in a bucket of cool water for a few moments and then walked across the store to fetch a broom and dust pan to clean up the mess.

Promptly at 6:00 p.m., Mr. Wright locked and turned the sign on the front door to CLOSED. After pulling down the shade on the door, the pharmacist took both cash drawers into the back room. "You've done very well today, Bob. Only two mistakes. Good work.

"See you tomorrow at eight o'clock. On Saturdays, I also close at 6:00 p.m., but you'll be free to go at 12:30 p.m., after you've given me a break to eat my sandwich."

"Thank you, sir. See you tomorrow."

Returning to his upstairs room, Bob lit his lamp and got some supper. Relaxing with a cup of hot tea and a scone for dessert, Bob thought about his first day of work and compared it to what he and Jim usually did on the farm. *It took me a long time before I could do everything well there. I guess I shouldn't expect to do everything perfectly here right away.*

Memories of Sam Pollack, the itinerant pitcher from Ontario, came flooding back. Bob thought about the way Sam had done his work in the fields and the way in which the man had related to and cared about the people around him. *Will I ever be able to develop such a heart? One that will-ingly serves and readily cares for others? I think I have a long way to go.*

Still mulling over his questions, Bob turned and stared at the dirty dishes from three meals. *Well, they won't clean themselves*, he thought. *But it'll be difficult to wash them up here.*

He flipped a dish towel over his shoulder, stuffed every dirty item and the oil tank from his room's stove into his largest pot, and carried it and his lamp downstairs to the soda fountain. Lighting his lamp and switching tanks on the stove, he did his dishes. Leaving the oil tank, his clean dishes, and his snuffed lamp at the foot of the stairs, he took the waste water to the outhouse and then locked the empty metal pans inside the back door. *Time for another stroll*, he thought. *This time I'll scout the part of town north of the railroad tracks.*

———◆———

Saturday morning, Mr. Wright had Bob unpacking and making inventory lists of new merchandise, stocking shelves, writing up and mailing orders for additional store supplies, and waiting on customers. It seemed some tasks were daily: sweeping, waiting on customers, and polishing display case and front door windows. Others were weekly: stocking shelves, dusting, polishing the large front store windows, arranging their displays, bottling and labelling Mr. Wright's various concoctions of remedies for common ailments. But apparently his main responsibility was soda jerk for an hour and a half after school Monday through Fridays and Saturday mornings.

———◆———

Just before his dinner time Saturday, Bob learned he was free until Tuesday morning, his first day of high school. Facing over forty-eight hours alone in a strange place, having no twin brother to do anything with, and knowing only two people in town, Bob wondered how he could fill the empty hours. For the first time in his life, he felt loneliness sink down to the bottom of his being. Growing up in a busy household with six siblings and almost nonstop work, he had longed for time alone to "hear himself think" and to read quietly ... without interruptions. Now that he had what he had wished for all his life, he wasn't sure what to do with it. *I've always believed an education would require a lot of personal sacrifice, but I guess I never anticipated this,* Bob thought. *Should I hike the twelve miles home, or should I visit the only other person I know in town?*

Later in the afternoon, Bob hesitated at the vicar's study door in the back of the church sanctuary. It'd been almost four years since his last visit—to return a book. There was a rustling and the scraping of a chair. The door opened before he knocked.

"Ah, young Robert," Reverend Wood said, "I've been expecting you. Earlier this week, Jack told me you were his new assistant and roomer. I put in a good word for you."

"Thank you, sir!"

"Come in. Have a seat. Looks like your father changed his mind at last. How did that happen?"

Bob told his friend about his struggle with despair, his discussions with Sam Pollack, his prayer to invite Jesus into his life, and his new sense of joy and hope. He also told of his wait for a Wood Lake School teacher with a high school certificate, his successful study for and passing of the ninth grade, and his father's recent change of heart. "But Pa said I had to do this on my own. Said he couldn't help me."

"Who in your family supports your move?"

"My mother. She's given me so many things for my bachelor living. Plus I know she prays for me every day."

"Not to discount the first, but the second is probably the best kind of support she could give you."

"Yes, I know." Bob smiled and added, "Perhaps my oldest brother, John, will support me too. He's the one who helped me move my things into my room above the store."

"That's good." Reverend Wood turned in his chair and studied the stack of books on the top of his desk. "Since you have some time and no studies yet, you'd probably like to borrow something to read." Handing Bob a well-worn volume, the vicar said, "One of my favourites."

"*Pilgrim's Progress* by John Bunyan," Bob read from its handsome, leather spine.

"This book is an allegory," Reverend Wood said. "So many times as I read it I thought the author was telling my story. Christian, the main character, is a young man who faces troubles, temptations, and sometimes detours through life. As you read the book, try to anticipate whether he will succeed or fail, and when he does succeed, think about why."

"Thanks for the book. Living in town will make it easier for me to return it. One more thing ..."

"Yes, Robert?"

"I've wished all my life for time alone. Some quiet. So I can read without interruption. So I have space for thinking."

"Now you have what you wished for." Reverend Wood looked at Robert over his glasses. "I hear a but ..."

Bob grimaced. "Right again. I guess I never anticipated how lonely I would feel after I had gotten my wish."

Reverend Wood nodded.

"Until two days ago, I spent my days with family and most hours with Jim. In spare moments now, I wonder what Jim is doing or what is happening on the farm. It's like living in two places at once."

"Are you questioning your decision to leave the farm? Your move to town?" the vicar asked. "Are you doubting your desire to finish high school?"

"No. To build my future I need to do all these things."

"Then give yourself time to get use to your new life. Take every concern you have about your brother, your family, your daily challenges to the Lord in prayer. Remember He has enabled you to be here. He is only a thought or a breath away."

Bob blinked. *Didn't I recently read the same idea in my Bible?* "Thanks, Reverend Wood."

"Robert, if you've nothing else planned for tomorrow, I'm inviting you to come to our worship service. It starts at 11:00 a.m. There's an evening service as well at 7:00. After the evening service, a half dozen young people meet together. You'd be welcome to join them."

"What do they do?"

"Come and find out."

"Alright, I will," Bob said, rising. "Better let you finish your sermon preparation."

Reverend Wood chuckled. "Good idea."

———————

The next two days passed quickly. Bob found the Anglican worship and evening services a lot more formal than he was used to. After the evening service, he joined the other teens in the fellowship hall in the church's basement. Much to Bob's relief, the boys who had laughed at him weren't part of the group. Instead, he met several other teens with whom he would be sharing his classes. Bob relaxed and enjoyed the activities. There was singing, a group discussion on a Bible passage led by Mrs. Wood, and treats provided by one of the girls in the group.

Much of the weekend, Bob practiced typing on sheets of brown wrapping paper in the back office. *Mr. Wright types without looking at the keys. He must have memorized them. But how? Their order makes no sense to me.* Bob also remembered the pharmacist using all ten fingers to type. After struggling to get his fourth and fifth fingers to strike keys with enough force, Bob gave up. *Only my first and second fingers and my thumbs are strong enough.* Using a hunt and peck method and four fingers, Bob worked at learning the order of the typewriter's keys.

Revelling in his first experience of uninterrupted time to read, Bob took off his shoes, put his feet on his bed, leaned back in his chair, and devoured page after page of Reverend Wood's book. Relating to all of the main character Christian's troubles was easy. And as Bob read, he wondered, *Which temptations will I face this year?*

chapter nineteen

Cherry Creek High School Student

The first day of high school finally came. Bob woke early, swept the store, and then splashed along two blocks of muddy streets through a downpour to the stone school. Dashing into the foyer, he almost ran into another student who was standing just inside the door.

"Oh, hi, McRuer," the teenager said.

"Hi, Russell. Call me Bob, would you?"

"Alright, Bob. I'm glad to see you. You were able to come after all!"

Bob smiled. "It's a miracle. I have a part-time job and a room at Wright's Drugstore."

"So you're living in town too! That's great!" Russel slapped Bob on his back. "My pa's made arrangements for me at Mrs. Gilbert's boarding house. He pays for my room and board there. You'll have to come visit sometime."

Russell and Bob were soon joined by groups of other students. The rain had forced everyone inside.

When the headmaster's office opened, Bob stood in line to get his schedule. From 8:00 to 10:00, he had Mr. Laing for Reading, Composition, Rhetoric, Literature, Grammar, Geography of the British Colonies, and English Constitutional History. Mr. Cottingham was his teacher from 10:00 to noon for Euclid's Plane Geometry and Experimental Chemistry. After an hour at noon for dinner, he had two more hours of classes, one for Drawing or Music and the other with Mr. Cottingham again for Animal Life.

Russell compared his schedule with Bob's. "I took Animal Life last year," Russell said, "but I have French II this year. That's where our schedules are different. You've already passed the French. Why don't you take Latin?"

"Aargh. What are you trying to do? Kill me?" Bob objected. "I'm looking at this list of subjects and wondering how I'm going to do all this and work part-time."

"It's not as bad as it looks," Russell consoled his new classmate and friend. "You won't have every subject every day. Some will be once a week, some two days, a few three."

"Which do you think will be three days a week?"

"Literature, History, Geometry, Chemistry, and Animal Life. Why do you ask?"

"Because they'll probably demand the most homework."

"Have you met our teachers yet?"

"No."

"Let's go then." Russell led Bob upstairs to their first class.

As Bob slid into a seat behind his friend, he heard whispers coming from the back of the room. When he turned to look, he saw the same teens who had taunted him at the soda fountain. Their look of surprise gave him great satisfaction. *My presence in this class isn't the only thing that will surprise you fellas this year. I'll show you a person from a farm has as many brains as you.*

At 8:00 a.m. promptly, their teacher began opening exercises, introduced himself, and asked each student to do the same. It was soon apparent to Bob that of the twenty-two students in their classroom, fourteen were tenth graders and eight were eleventh graders. All but two of the students came from families who lived in or near the town.

According to their individual introductions, Russell and Bob were the only ones who were boarding or rooming in Cherry Creek while their families were on farms miles away. In spite of the fact that Russell was his junior by years, Bob felt he had more in common with the short, spindly fifteen year old than any of his other classmates.

Russell's prediction about the weekly routine proved true. The most demanding subjects Bob had several times a week. Others only one or two. Another factor complicated things for Bob. Each hour of the school day, the tenth graders shared their classroom and their teacher with the eleventh graders. He figured out very quickly that on the days Mr. Cottingham taught trigonometry to the eleventh graders, he could concentrate on his geometry homework better if he used a pass to the school's library/music room.

Music classes included students from all three high school grades: ninth, tenth, and eleventh. Three days a week Bob stumbled through "do, re, me, fa, sol, la, ti, do" in two or three different keys under the direction of Mrs. Ashley, a local church organist and choir director. Although he surprised himself and his teacher with his decent baritone, he had a terrible time with the music class. Mother had given his sister, Jessie, hours of music instruction, but never him—since he'd shown no interest. Now he regretted not haven taken advantage of Mother's musical expertise.

———

Being soda jerk after school turned out to be the worst part of each day. The teens who had taunted Bob his first day of work brought others from his class to park themselves on the stools of the soda fountain. They noisily demanded service. Through conversations with each other at the counter, a few of the boys bragged about their prowess at the after-school sports activities, rubbing it in that Bob couldn't participate because he had to work.

During each soda jerk session, Bob gritted his teeth, struggling to keep his balled up fists at his side. *I thought when I became Bob and was no longer Allister, there wouldn't be any more teasing. I can't believe this. I feel like I am right back where I started from—face to face with my lifelong nemesis.* He was well aware the old Allister, with no leash on his temper at all, would've pounded the daylights out of a couple of boys in some back alley when they least expected it.

At closing on a day the teenage boys had been particularly mean, Mr. Wright suggested he and Bob talk for a bit when he brought the soda fountain's cash drawer to the back room. "Bob, a few of those boys are giving you a rough time, aren't they?"

"Yes, sir."

"Remember that if you respect yourself and treat others with respect, they'll eventually treat you with respect."

"Yes, sir. Thank you, Mr. Wright."

"Plus I have another suggestion. On Saturday afternoons, some of those same boys practice football on a field near the school. Volunteer to help them scrimmage. Here's a leather belt to hold up your pants. Suspenders don't work on a football field."

"I know, sir." Bob grinned. "We had a few pants-down incidents at Wood Lake School last year when we tried tackle football. Thanks for the suggestion."

———◆———

The very next Saturday afternoon, Bob went to the field Mr. Wright had told him about. Since no one was there when he arrived, he lay down in the grass at the edge of the field and studied the clouds. A group of boys eventually showed up with a football. Bob sat up to watch the team selection. When three of the troublemakers ended up on the same team, Bob got up and volunteered to play on the opposite side. "Alright, Bob, you can play, but you'll have to be a linebacker," the captain of his team said.

Watching carefully for the intended receiver, Bob plowed through the opposing linemen at each snap of the ball. Wham! Bob flattened the teen carrying the ball. By the end of the scrimmage, each of the troublemakers had met up with Bob's six feet of bulk, muscle, and determination several times.

As he walked away later, he muttered to himself, "That was more fun than punching their lights out." Flexing his arms and back and rubbing his shoulders, slightly sore from the repeated hits during the scrimmage, Bob thought about the Bible verse he had stumbled across that very morning: *"He that is slow to anger is better than the mighty; and he that ruleth his spirit than he that taketh a city."*[15]

When Bob was finally ready to sit down at his desk in his room above the now silent drugstore, he looked at his clock and gasped. *Oh boy. An afternoon of teaching my taunters a lesson ate up study time. How will I ever get all of my geometry and chemistry homework done?*

chapter twenty

Bachelor Survival

T he last Thursday night of September, Russell sat in Bob's room above the drugstore. The next day they had their first tests in chemistry and geometry. Bob had already studied for the tests, so he was quizzing Russell on the applications of their maxims in geometric proofs, the elements of the periodic table, and the chemical formulas for air, water, salt, and sugar. Russell couldn't seem to memorize it all.

"How much time have you been spending with your books every night, my friend?" Bob finally had to ask. He suspected the answer was next to zero.

"Not much. Just enough to get the homework written. How much do you do?"

"At least three, sometimes four hours. And another four or five on Saturdays."

"Gee! Don't you give yourself any time off?"

"Of course. A few hours on Saturday afternoon for football scrimmage and all day Sunday. The important key is to study the new concepts and vocabulary every day and review the old often. I learned to prepare for tests ahead of time while I was attending Wood Lake School. Well, hate to kick you out, but I've got to get to bed. Have to sweep out the store before school tomorrow."

"Are you going home for the Thanksgiving holiday this weekend?"

"Of course. Wouldn't miss it."

Before Bob left for home Saturday, he asked Mr. Wright for some of his pay. When the pharmacist had hired him a month ago, he made no mention of when he would pay Bob. He thought he'd waited long enough. His boss gave him $5.00 and promised to pay him the rest when he came back to work on Tuesday.

Dreading the long hike home in a breeze with a definite nip to it, Bob promptly walked over to Nicol's General Store to buy a cap for fifty cents. While he was there, he saw a number of things he needed but only paid an additional thirty-five cents—for a dish pan.

About three o'clock he was able to beg a ride with a driver heading south from the grain elevator. An hour later, he thanked the driver at the next main intersection and strode east on the road which would take him through Desford and home. Thinking, *Gotta get home before dark,* he picked up his pace.

Bob was hustling past the general store in the little town when he saw Georgie and his father, Thomas. *It would be great if they would help me out.* Calling to them, Bob begged a ride. Answering the younger boy's questions one after the other, Bob told all about life in Cherry Creek. Before he knew it, their horses had trotted the four and a half miles of road to the end of the McRuer farm lane. Bob thanked Thomas and climbed down from the wagon seat.

Only a faint glow fringed the western horizon as Bob strode towards his family's farmhouse. Tawny's excited barking greeted him before he even got to the house.

Scooting Tawny back, Mother hugged Bob while he was still standing in the doorway. "Welcome home, son. I was hoping you'd make it."

John dried his hands and hung the towel on the wash stand. "Made it before dark. That's good. How long did it take you to get home?"

"I left Cherry Creek about three o'clock." Bob pulled Pa's watch out of a pocket and flipped open its cover. "Goodness. It's only a quarter to six!"

"Then you didn't have to walk all the way," John said.

"No, got a couple of rides."

Mother placed a steaming platter of cooked carrots and sliced roast beef next to a pan of scalloped potatoes on the table. "Supper's ready. Everyone sit."

"Looks wonderful!" Bob licked his lips. *A home-cooked meal. Nothing could be better.* "Mother, are Dan and Will coming for Thanksgiving?"

"Dan promised to. Will wrote he doesn't have enough time off to make the trip for Thanksgiving, but plans to come for Christmas."

"Son, you have to go back to town Monday night, don't you?" Father asked. When Bob nodded, Father added, "There'll be no freight wagons to catch a ride on. Monday's a holiday."

Oh, right. Bob thought. *It never occurred to me that getting back would be harder than getting home.*

During supper, Jessie and Jim asked some of the same questions Georgie had. Father ate in silence. Mother and John just smiled at the exchange between the three youngest members of the family.

While Bob was sharing his experiences with his family, his emotions swung wildly. On the one hand, he was ecstatic. He had achieved what he had waited for so many years—to leave home so he could attend high school. On the other hand, he had been so homesick. It took coming home for him to realize how much. *I haven't wanted to admit it even to myself. Church at Wood Lake School on Sunday, just like years past. Spending time with Mother and Jim. So good. I've missed them the most,* Bob thought. *Even if this visit includes two days of pitching the foul-smelling straw from the barn stalls.*

"How have things been going?" Bob asked Jim as they worked together Sunday evening.

"Well, we really missed you during harvest, Allister."

Bob frowned. *Allister? Jim called me Allister. How am I going to undo that family habit of calling me by my middle name?*

Jim tossed a forkful of dirty straw into a wheelbarrow. "With harvest finished, the four of us at home have worked out a routine. Dan's busy at his own place. Although John still lives here, he's spending more and more time on his own claim. He's quarrying rock from Turtle Mountain and hauling it to his homestead."

"Quarrying rock? What for?" Bob asked.

"His house."

That can't be any less work than making and laying bricks, Bob thought. *McRuers never do things the easy way.*

He gulped. *Might as well start the retraining of the naming habit with my twin.* "Jim, remember calling me 'Bob, the log' that day on the river near Killarney?"

"Yep." Jim chuckled.

"Well, I'd like you to call me Bob. It's what everyone in town is calling me."

"Alright, Bob," Jim said, grinning and slapping his twin on the back. "Anything to get rid of Allis, right?"

"Exactly."

————◆————

On the morning of Thanksgiving Day, John lounged around the house, and Dan joined them shortly after breakfast.

Happy for a chance to talk with two of his older brothers, Bob said, "I was hoping I would get to see you, Dan."

"Mother made us both promise to be here Thanksgiving Day," John said.

"Besides, we couldn't let the family's perpetual student get away without taking his October quiz," Dan teased.

"My quiz?" Bob frowned. "What do you mean?'

"How many students does it take to harvest a field of wheat?" Dan asked.

"Hmm. Don't know."

"You just failed your quiz." Dan winked at John. "The answer is none. You weren't here, and we did it without you."

"Ha, ha, Dan," Bob said. "Very funny."

"What has life in town been like?" Dan asked.

And the story swapping began.

Monday's Thanksgiving meal had never tasted so delicious to Bob. Like his father when he left their Quebec farm to start their homestead claim in Manitoba ten years ago, Bob was no cook. He was surviving his bachelor life in Cherry Creek mostly because of Mother's "care crates." On a Saturday morning two weeks ago, she'd dropped by Wright's Drugstore with additional supplies. After the family's Thanksgiving meal, his mother told Bob she'd send him back to town with more.

"Mother, getting back would be a whole lot easier for me if you'd let me borrow Shalazar and the buggy," Bob begged. "I'll pay to board him at the livery stable in town until you can pick him up on your next trip to town."

"I won't be coming until next Saturday," Mother said, looking worried. "Tell you what, I'll split the cost with you. Alright?"

"That would be great!"

"Remember, son, any mending or laundry can be sent home in an empty packing crate whenever John, Jim, or I drop off supplies for you at Wright's."

"Thank you so much, Mother."

Late Monday afternoon, when Mother brought out the items for him to load in the buggy, Bob noticed a brand-new shirt folded and lying on top of the supplies in a crate. Kissing her on the cheek and bending over to give Jessie a hug and Tawny a pat, Bob gratefully took the reins from Jim.

Shalazar, in a hurry as always, trotted into Cherry Creek in a little over an hour. Dropping his boxes off inside the back door of the drugstore, Bob drove Mother's horse a block over to the livery stable. Leaving the horse and two days board with the manager, Bob returned to the drugstore and carried his boxes of supplies up to his room.

After lighting his lamp, Bob slumped into a chair. Putting his elbows on the desk and chin in his hands, his solitude pressed in on him. *Too quiet. That's Cherry Creek after dark. Alone once more. The silence seems louder. Going home and being with family was so good for me. Except when I come back to town, I am more homesick than I was two days ago. Don't feel like studying tonight—or reading my Bible. Go to bed early. Maybe after a good night's sleep, things will look better. Need to unpack the boxes of supplies first.*

At the bottom of the box with the shirt, Bob found a sad-iron. Under the iron was a note. He read:

Dear Son,
I've sewn you a new shirt. It is clean and pressed this time. But from now on—press your own clothes.
Love, Mother

Bob smiled and shook his head. *I have no idea how to iron anything. One more thing to learn how to do. Better not practice on my new shirt, though. I'll probably burn the first item I try to iron.*

——◆——

As winter settled over the town, Bob had new conditions with which he had to cope. Although Mother tried to bring supplies from home every week or two, or he tried to make trips home some weekends, at times neither happened. When he ran short of supplies, he had to stretch his earnings. Bread enough for five days cost twenty-five cents. Coal oil for his cabinet stove was thirty-five cents. Then there were school fees of $2 or $3 every couple of months and books for his literature course to buy. The haircut his mother usually gave him now seemed old fashioned, so he reluctantly shelled out twenty-five cents for his first cut at the local barbershop. As his boots wore out and his pants got too short, he had to replace them—boots at $2.25 and $2.75 for pants.

Earning between $5 and $6 as a monthly average, Bob kept a detailed account in a cash journal of each cent earned and spent. His goal was to have some money left over at the end of each month. Bob soon discovered his wages, more than he had ever earned before, were barely adequate to cover the necessaries no matter how careful he was.

Other problems presented themselves. Unlike the farmhouse's room directly above the kitchen's wood-burning cook stove, Bob's upper room at the drugstore was unheated. During December and January, dressing in the morning became torture, and bathing impossible. His only escape was to run in stocking feet, clothes in hand, to the basement. Dressing next to the coal furnace after stoking it every morning seemed the only way to warm up—that and drinking hot tea and eating boiled oatmeal for breakfast.

Sitting for hours in a room where one could see one's breath was another challenge. Bob remembered his mother's heated wheat pillow for Jessie's puppy, Tawny. Borrowing a hot water bottle at night from a drugstore display case, Bob filled it with hot water and sat with its warmth tucked against his stomach under his sweater. The stiffness of his frosted fingers was somewhat alleviated by a pair of gloves without their fingertips Mother had knit for him as a Christmas present.

John had given Bob a wonderful gift then as well—four rabbit skins from his Turtle Mountain traps. Borrowing a large needle from Mother and scissors from the wrapping station in the store, Bob cut and sewed a pair of fur-lined slippers. They were a rough replica of the moccasins Sammy's mother, Stalking Deer, had made for him in early winter when the boy had been Bob's classmate at Wood Lake School.

In January, the bitter cold in his upper room got too much for Bob. At the end of a school day, he waited for Russell in the central hallway. "Hey, Russ, could I come over after supper tonight? The frost in my room freezes my thoughts as well as my fingers."

"Hmm, wonder what frozen thoughts look like," Russell chuckled. "Sure, come. Mrs. Gilbert says I can have any fellas over, but no girls."

"Thanks. Want help with your French?"

"Umm, alright. Could use some. One more thing … my landlady says all visitors must leave by 10:00 p.m. See you."

Bathing in such frigid conditions took a little creativity too. Bob remembered Mother's "bathhouse" next to her kitchen stove. Taking his blankets, teakettle of hot water, a dish pan, and clean clothes to the basement, he hung the blankets from the ceiling joists close to the furnace to make a heated chamber. In it, he gave himself a scrub down.

His chamber pot in the frost-bitten mornings was another matter. Bob often left it to thaw on the furnace while he was sweeping the drugstore's main floor. Before he left for school each morning, Bob would retrieve the thawed chamber pot and toss its contents into the outhouse behind the store.

One noon, however, when Bob came back to the drugstore for his dinner break, Mr. Wright complained about how badly his store stunk. Several customers had left the store holding their noses.

"I can't figure out where the smell's coming from," the pharmacist said.

One sniff and Bob knew. Running downstairs, he checked the top of the furnace. Sure enough, he'd forgotten to empty the chamber pot. The heat had been boiling its odors throughout the building for hours.

After removing the "stinker," Bob remembered to stoke the furnace before he trudged up the stairs with the pot. *What will Mr. Wright say? Will he be angry? My forgetfulness cost him business this morning. Will he ask me to find another place to live? Perhaps fire me?*

When Bob appeared with the container in hand, Mr. Wright laughed. "So that's the culprit?"

Astounded, Bob stood rooted to the spot near the back door of the store. *He laughed. He isn't mad.* Bob's anxiety vanished.

"Yes, sir," he replied. "Sorry. Won't happen again!"

Running up to his room with a rinsed and emptied chamber pot several minutes later, Bob muttered. "Oh brother. What else can go wrong?"

chapter twenty-one

Medical Mishaps

L oud banging on Bob's door one night in late January startled him awake. Stumbling across the cold floor in his bare feet, he opened the door to a frantic Mr. Wright.

"Bob, I gave a woman the wrong medicine. While I redo the compound, dress warm and fetch my horse from the livery stable. I am asking *you* to make the emergency delivery."

"Sir, I don't know which horse is yours."

"A stable hand sleeps there. Wake him up. He'll get my horse for you."

Bob yanked on layers of his warmest clothes. At the stable, he had to shake awake the person in charge. "Please saddle Mr. Wright's horse. We have an emergency delivery to make."

"Alright. Be ready in a minute."

At the back door of the drugstore, Bob checked and tightened the cinch on the horse's saddle.

Inside, Mr. Wright showed Bob a bottle and a paper package. "The correct medication is in the bottle. The dosage instructions are on the bottle label. Use the contents of the paper package only if the woman has given her husband the other medication already. The instruction for its use is written on it. Its contents are designed to make him vomit up the other medication. Stay with Mrs. Dirksen until you are sure she can follow all my directions. The Dirksens are Ukrainian immigrants. They live ..."

"If you mean Sofi and Dietrich Dirksen, I know where they live!"

"Yes, I do. Good man! Now put this on." Mr. Wright handed Bob a pocketed cloth belt into which he had buttoned the medications.

At the back door, the pharmacist reached for the horse's reins. "One last piece of advice, young man. Wrap at least one hand in Lightning's mane. He's young, strong, and loves to run!"

After taking an extra second to tie his cap down with his scarf, Bob swung up on Lightning. With the clank of iron-clad hooves on frozen ground, his mount bolted onto the main trail heading south. A mile from town they clattered across the newly-built Pembina River Bridge. Lightning lived up to his name. Seeming to understand the urgency of his mission, the horse stretched into a dead run and reached the intersection of the roads seven miles out in half the usual time.

Reining his mount in, Bob leaned left. Lightning took the cue and wheeled left. Streaking through Desford, the horse would've continued the race east if Bob hadn't pulled him down to a slow trot in time to turn into the Dirksen's farm lane. The horse headed straight for the back door of the house and stood puffing with his head down, as if he knew his job was done and he could rest.

Bob jumped to the ground and pounded on the door. *Hope we're not too late.*

Sofi opened it, looking dumbfounded to see him. In an instant, Lucy stood right behind her mother.

"Allis-sir!" Lucy stared at him with wide eyes. "Is middle of night. Why you here?"

"Mr. Wright sent me with new medicine for your father, Lucy. Sofi, did you give Dietrich his medicine yet?"

"No," Sofi said when Lucy had translated. "I not give him medicine."

Relief washed over Bob. "Very good. Mr. Wright gave you the wrong medicine. He made new medicine. Here it is."

After fumbling with the buttons on the belt around his waist, Bob drew out the bottle, handed it to Sofi, and asked Lucy to give him back the other one. When he had the wrong compound in hand, he said, "Excuse me a minute. Need to put Mr. Wright's horse in your barn. Then I'll come in a minute."

"Ya. Ya. Come in mein haus," Sofi said.

Bob tied Lightning in an empty stall, making sure there was no water or hay within reach. He didn't want the sweaty horse to get sick.

When Bob re-entered the Dirksen's house, he was struck by the spotless, whitewashed, plastered walls of the kitchen and the delicate, blue stitching on the white curtains in its one window. What a contrast to the mud brown walls of the Soddy the family had been living in when they first came to Manitoba! Bob no longer wondered about the reason for Sofi's depression Mother had told him about!

"Mr. Wright told me to show you how to give Dietrich the medicine. Lucy, please get a big cup of water."

When the girl returned with the water, Bob read the dosage directions on the label out loud. Putting the correct amount of medicine in Sofi's hand, Bob made sure she understood how much and when to give it.

"Ya, Gut! Danke," Sofi said.

Bob talked briefly with Dietrich and then followed Lucy and Sofi back into the kitchen. "I give you coffee now," Sofi said.

Sipping the bitter, black liquid, Bob couldn't help making a face.

"You like coffee no very much, Allis-sir?" Lucy observed.

"Not really."

"Give me your cup. I make better."

The girl put some cream and honey in it and stirred it.

"Better?" she asked after Bob had tasted it.

"Yes, better! Thank you. Lucy, please call me Bob. Bob will be easier for you and Hilda to say. Easier than Allister, right?" Bob smiled as he remembered the difficulty all the Dirksens had in pronouncing his name ever since they arrived a little over a year ago.

Lucy laughed. "Ya. Bob. Easy."

"Sofi, Lucy, thanks for the coffee. Hope Dietrich gets better soon."

"Ya. Velcome. Tank medicine man and tank you for better medicine you bring. Gut night."

Bob led Lightning down the farm lane to the road. First the hot coffee and now the walk were warming him up. Meanwhile, the frosty air cooled off the horse. "Well, Lightning, you rescued a man tonight. You know that, don't you, boy?"

Lightning snorted and bobbed his head.

"My brother Dan says he's sure some horses speak English. Maybe you're one of them."

At this, Lightning stopped, shook his head, and pawed the ground.

"Alright, I get it. Time to run home."

Bob mounted and rode at an easy, rolling canter all the way to the livery stable.

"Looks like you know how to take care of your mount," the stable hand said when Bob handed the horse over to him. "Mr. Wright usually returns him lathered."

"What a good boy!" Bob patted the horse.

Turning towards the stable hand, he added, "Don't give me credit for knowing the right thing to do. I simply followed my brother John's advice. Thank you for taking good care of Lightning. Good night, sir."

———◆———

A few weeks later, Bob had another surprise. Tooth twinges turned into one gigantic ache. It got so bad, he couldn't study and could hardly chew anything.

"Mr. Wright, I've had a horrible toothache for several days now," Bob said as they closed up the drugstore one evening. "But no idea what to do about it."

"Ever had any dental work done?" the pharmacist asked.

"Dental? No. Mother helped me pull out my baby teeth when they got loose, but that's it."

"Ever brushed your teeth?"

Bob frowned. *People brush their teeth as well as their hair?* "No."

"Which tooth hurts?"

"Well, there are actually two teeth that hurt. One here and another there," Bob said, opening his mouth and pointing.

"Come over here." The pharmacist walked behind the main counter and reached for a tiny bottle. "Lay the tip of this toothpick against the gum at the base of the hurting tooth." He handed the small stick to Bob after dipping it into the bottle.

Bob's taste buds twanged and the pain in his tooth subsided. "What's that?" he asked, pointing at the bottle.

"Oil of clove. It's a strong flavouring, but it can also numb your toothaches temporarily. Apply it now and again until you can see Dr. Shaffner about filling the cavities you probably have in your teeth."

"Dr. Shaffner? But he's a doctor. Takes care of people's bodies."

"As the area's only doctor, he has to take care of teeth too."

———

Several days later, Bob asked his teacher, Mr. Cottingham, to excuse him from his last two classes of the morning so the doctor could work on his teeth. The doctor gave Bob nitrous oxide gas to make the tooth drilling and filling less painful. The gas left a sweet taste in Bob's mouth and made him giddy before it put him to sleep. When Bob woke up, he was dizzy. Walking back from the doctor's office could only be managed by putting a hand on the buildings to steady his amble along the streets.

"How did it go?" Mr. Wright said when Bob entered the store.

"Terrible!" Bob mumbled.

"What did the doc do?"

"Filled each cavity with something he called silver amalgam. Cost $2.00."

"You look like you need to sleep off the pain killer he gave you. Don't worry about classes or the soda fountain. I'll take care of everything."

"Thank you, sir."

Bob stumbled upstairs and plopped onto his bed. When he woke up it was already dark outside, but his toothaches were gone and he was starving. Even then he decided to be gentle on his mouth. Lighting his lamp and turning on his stove, he fixed himself a poached egg on a slice of bread that had been soaked in warm milk.

Delighted the pain in his mouth was gone, Bob filled a hot water bottle to warm himself and settled in to study for several hours.

Unfortunately, one of the fillings proved to be a temporary fix. Six weeks later, the toothache returned. When Bob saw Dr. Shaffner the second time about the same tooth, they decided the tooth should be pulled. Bob was relieved it would only cost fifty cents.

"Before you give me the nitrous oxide gas again, I'd like to ask you if I might come back some time to talk to you. After I finish high school, I want to be a doctor. Maybe you can tell me something about how to become one."

"I'd be happy to. What grade are you in now?"

"Tenth grade."

"That's good. Work for Jack after school, don't you?"

"Yes, sir."

"When will you have some free time?"

"Saturday afternoons."

"Alright. Stop by next Saturday."

"Thank you, sir."

The month of May and exam preparation came soon enough. Russell and William, another classmate, formed a threesome with Bob to study for hours and hours.

When the testing days arrived the last week of June, he was ready. Having been through the process before, he knew more what to expect. When the results were posted, he was delighted he had passed everything again, although he wished his Geometry score was a little higher. Bob was also happy Russell had done better this year than last. Bob's last school activity for the year was to pay the required $5.00 fee and receive his tenth grade certificate during the program to close the school year.

Bob's final day at the drugstore was the last Saturday of June.

"Bob," Mr. Wright said, "you were an excellent employee and roomer. The job and the room are yours for next fall if you're planning on returning."

"Thank you, sir. I will."

The very next day was Sunday, July 1, Dominion Day. Bob's family came to town to enjoy Canada's annual celebration and move him home for the summer.

During the ride home, Bob thought about several huge volumes resting in the bottom of one of his crates—medical books Dr. Shaffner had lent him. Unwilling to let summer interrupt his progress, Bob thought, *How am I going to get the time necessary to absorb what's in those tomes? There is so much to learn.*

chapter twenty-two

A Word of Encouragement

aving tasted a bit of community life with other teens in town, Bob grew impatient with life on the farm. *My social activity out here is limited mostly to my family. While I love my family and I am grateful for everything they, especially my mother, have given or done for me, I believe there is more to life than what's here on the farm. I've already proved to myself, at least, that I am capable of doing more.*

Summer days dragged their heels for Bob. Other than a couple of fishing trips with Jim and John, the long days were spent working in fields and garden or quarrying and hauling split boulders from Turtle Mountain for John's house and barn foundation.

Each evening, Bob ended a full day of field work with the study of a chapter in his Bible and sampling from the books of British poets and Shakespeare's plays that Reverend Wood had lent him. Hesitant to openly declare his intentions to go to medical school after finishing high school, Bob usually spent time with Dr. Shaffner's medical books after everyone else had gone to bed. *I guess I am hoping the presence of these books on top of Mother's hutch in the dining room will make Pa and John aware of my interest.*

———◆———

Relieved when August 31 finally came, Bob moved with Jim's help back into the room above Wright's Drugstore. He was more than ready to work the next day.

Now in his second year at the drugstore, it was obvious from the first day that Mr. Wright would give Bob more responsibility for the inventories, ordering, general bookkeeping, counting the cash drawers, and putting the correct quantities of change in them. "Bob, you already know how to package and label. This year, I'd also like you to help me keep up my stock of cough syrup, ointments, liniments, and headache powders. I'll teach you how to measure and mix the compounds."

"That'll be great, sir. I'll do my best," Bob said, thinking, *Finally, I'll get to learn what it means to be a pharmacist. Better make sure I use the correct ingredients and measure accurately. Won't soon forget the frightening midnight ride to the Dirksens' to replace a bottle of wrong medicine with the right one.*

"Bob, would it be possible for you to use all ten of your fingers when you type labels? Instead of just two on each hand? Your typing speed would improve considerably, you know!"

Bob laughed. "You did say to teach myself how to type, didn't you? Well, I have. You haven't seen any mistakes on my typed labels, have you, Mr. Wright?"

"No, Bob. I guess you have a method that works for you."

———◆———

Knowing he would be totally on his own for the next two days, Bob reminisced about the experiences of the previous year. *Yes, I will miss Mother's cooking. And spending time with Jim and John. Must remember I managed my daily life all the months of the previous school year without them. Besides, I know more people in Cherry Creek now. I'll be fine. I'll get use to this life again.*

During the Labour Day weekend, Bob used the time to get reacquainted with the congregation and youth group at Reverend Wood's church. On Monday afternoon, he went to see Russell McKinnon. When Bob dropped by Russell's usual boarding place, his landlady said he was out for a walk. Cherry Creek wasn't big. Bob figured if he walked enough blocks, he'd run into his friend. After several blocks, he saw the teen down a side street walking with …a girl! Running to catch up, Bob joined their promenade.

"Hi, Bob." Russell turned to the girl. "Gwen, this is my friend, Bob."

"Hello, Gwen," Bob said, shaking hands with the blue-eyed, blonde-headed slip of a girl. "I'm glad to meet you. Weren't you one of the eighth-grade graduates last June?"

"Uh-huh," she said, smiling sweetly and looking bashfully up at Bob. "I'm in the ninth grade this year."

"Then you'll have most of the same teachers we do. Russ, is it alright if I walk with you?"

Russ looked at Gwen. When she nodded, he said, "Sure."

The three shared stories about their summer until it was almost suppertime and they were standing next to the white picket gate in front of Gwen's house.

"My mother's calling me," she said. "I'd better go in."

"See you tomorrow, Gwen." Russell opened the gate for her.

Bob accompanied Russell to his boarding house. "Are you thinking of squiring a girl this year, Russ?" Bob was amused at the thought.

"Why not? Gwen's a beautiful girl. She's kind-hearted and from a good family. But she's not the only one in town. There are quite a few others ... or haven't you noticed?"

"Of course I have! But ..."

"But what?"

"Isn't she a bit young to have a beau? Aren't you too? What's the hurry?"

"Relax, Bob, my man. I'm not serious about any one girl yet." Russell reached up to lay his hand on his tall friend's shoulder. "Besides, I don't have the big plans you do!"

"Big plans?"

"Uh-huh. I saw all those medical books on your desk last June. From Dr. Shaffner, eh? Spent the whole summer studying them too, I'd bet. Are you planning to be a doctor?"

"Umm, yes, if I can ever get to medical school." Bob sighed.

"Well, I hope you do, my friend!" Russell smiled. "See you tomorrow."

Several hours later, when Bob settled in for an evening of reading, he thought about Russell's comments. *He called my plans big. Guess he's right. Striving to not only finish high school but also get myself ready for something as tough as medical school has made me an intense, no nonsense student. Even from my first day of high school, being years older than all the other students made me different. Becoming a serious student because of my big dreams has simply widened the gap between me and my classmates ... come to think of it, between me and my family as well.*

If I were to slack off? Take it easier? Just to be more like the other high school students? I know I wouldn't have a chance to reach my goal. Gotta give myself a chance!

On the first day of the new school year, the hallway outside the headmaster's office was abuzz with more high school students than the previous year. Apparently in anticipation of the additional students, the secretary and a parent volunteer were seated at a table across from the office door to hand out class schedules and help students who were late registrants.

Once Bob and Russell both had their schedules in hand, they headed upstairs to their first classroom. Both teens had Mr. Laing again this year for eleventh-grade Reading, Composition and Rhetoric, Literature, Grammar, Physical Geography, and World History. Mr. Cottingham was the teacher for Plane Trigonometry for one hour of the morning and Mr. Laing for Latin the last hour of the day. But that's where the similarity ended. Russell had opted out of the Physics Bob was taking. And Bob had signed up for Physiology. "What are you doing during the fourth and fifth classes, Russ?"

"Repeating History of Canada to see if I can get a better grade in it. I'm also taking an additional year of Drawing and Music."

"I'd like to learn more music, but I don't have room in my schedule."

"Bob, you've signed up for every heavy subject there is!" Russ exclaimed.

"I had to. When I talked to Dr. Shaffner about my dreams of becoming a doctor, he said I'd have to go to medical school after high school. He also told me anything I learned about Latin, mathematics, and science, especially human anatomy, would help me handle those really tough medical courses."

"Don't you have to make really good marks just to get in?"

"Yes, of course. So far, so good!"

Russell smiled at his friend.

Maybe now Russ understands why I've been driving myself so hard, Bob thought. *I'm not a strange one. I'm a young man with a plan!*

———————

As the eleventh graders did their difficult dive into Shakespearean English, Bob discovered he had a distinct advantage. His love of poetry, his reading of *Pilgrim's Progress*, his consistent study of his King James Bible, and all the reading he had done over the summer helped him understand the complex English of the plays. All too often he was the student who could explain to his fellow students *Hamlet* and their other assigned readings of Shakespeare.

Just as he was a resource for others, he found people in the community who were willing resources for him. When Bob struggled with the math concepts in trigonometry, or those he needed to do the physics homework, Mr. Wright offered to help him. And it was Reverend Wood who often unravelled the complicated Latin grammar Bob tried to understand. But Dr. Shaffner and Mr. Wright were the most help in impressing on Bob just how important his Latin vocabulary was. Those two men showed him over and over how those Latin roots provided the basis for much of the medical and pharmaceutical vocabulary he'd be studying later.

To make things a little more difficult for Bob this year, Russell wasn't always available as a study buddy. The younger teen had two classes with Gwen and wasn't taking some of Bob's hardest courses. This forced him to find other students with whom to study, sometimes even one or two of the girls in his class.

The hour and a half of Bob's work as a soda jerk five days a week became his biggest trial … of his patience. As a young man who had worked so hard just to get to high school, he was appalled at the flippant, non-cooperative, ungrateful attitudes he was picking up from the conversations of the teens who frequently hung around the soda fountain after school. Since Bob had judiciously trounced a few of the fellows during football scrimmage last fall, they no longer gave him any trouble, almost treating him with a grudging respect. But Bob often had to bite his tongue to keep his viewpoints and counsel to himself.

"Hard to keep quiet sometimes," Mr. Wright said to Bob as they closed up one evening. "I can see you'd like to give them a piece of your mind a time or two. So would I. But it'd do those young people little good. They aren't ready to listen. Wait until one or two are. Then ask God to give you the right words to speak. The right word at the right time can change a life, Bob."

"I know what you mean, sir." Bob told his boss about Sam Pollack, the itinerant threshing crew member from Ontario, and the question he had asked Bob in his father's wheat field. "God used that brief, accidental contact with one man to change my life," Bob concluded.

When he looked up, he thought he saw the glint of a tear in Mr. Wright's eyes. "Young Bob, when you walked into my drugstore to ask for a job, I knew you were different. But I didn't know in what way, at the time. God will use you yet to bless many lives."

As Bob climbed the stairs to his room, he thought, *That's what I've needed from another man for a long time—encouragement and a belief in me. I wonder if either will ever come from my father or any of my brothers.*

chapter twenty-three

The Set Up

B ob didn't get his first pay until the end of October. It was a good thing his mother was faithful about bringing him food supplies and taking his laundry every other week. Since he now knew the freight wagon schedules and drivers, Bob could often catch a ride all the way to Desford before he had to complete the rest of the way home on foot. If he timed it right, he could usually catch a ride back, sometimes Sunday night, sometimes very early Monday.

As soon as he received $13.00 for his first two months of work at Wright's Drugstore, Bob bought some long underwear ($1.50), a pair of pants ($3.00), another cap (fifty cents), boots ($3.00), and overshoes ($2.00). He was glad he had already bought cufflinks for twenty cents, and a coat and vest for $5.00 last year when he had the money in the spring. After his newest clothing purchases, he had little left when he paid his $2.00 school fee. Bob was grateful when Mr. Wright didn't wait so long to give him his next pay of $5.00. Then there was enough to buy fresh bread (twenty-five cents) every couple of days. Luxuries such as a few apples for twenty-five cents and some butter for fifteen cents became possible once or twice a month.

In the spring, the one luxury he really wanted he wasn't sure he should pay for—a fee of fifteen cents to play on their school baseball team. The team practiced and played games once a week on Fridays, right after school. *Will Mr. Wright let me off to play baseball?* Bob wondered.

The next Friday while he was helping Mr. Wright close the drugstore, Bob brought up the subject. "My school is forming a baseball team this year," Bob said. "I'd like to play."

"Oh?"

"The team's going to practice and play on Fridays after school. Could I work more hours on Saturday in exchange for not working on Friday afternoons?"

"When does the team start its practices?"

"Next Friday."

"When is its last practice?"

"The second Friday of June."

"It'll continue for ten weeks then?"

"Yes, but our last game is on July 1."

"Alright, Bob. You can have Friday afternoons off. But I'll only let you make up one hour—by working on Saturday 'til 1:30 p.m."

Bob winced. That meant he'd lose an hour's pay a week. But this bargain gave him his first and maybe only chance to play a team sport.

"Thank you, sir!"

———————

The very next week Bob signed up, paid the fee, and went to practice. All the pop flies and line drives he'd caught from his twin's batting practice now paid off. At the first try outs, he landed the position of short stop. Excited, he ran to Russel's boarding house after practice to share his good news with his friend.

Realizing he wasn't in the best shape from all the months of sitting, Bob talked Russell into running around town with him right after school. He didn't have a lot of time, but a twenty-minute run four times a week should make a difference. Bob had to learn to shorten his stride a little to make it easier for Russell to keep up. After two weeks of running, Bob was no longer sweating or puffing when they finished. "Russ, why don't you join the team?" Bob asked when they stopped in front of Wright's Drugstore.

"Well, um, Friday games are something I can take Gwen to."

"Invite her to come watch you. It would give you a chance to escort her home afterwards. Besides, having her and a couple of her friends there to cheer us on might help us win a game, eh?"

"Yeah, alright. Bob, I was talking to Mr. Cottingham in drawing class the other day. He says drawing is part of the eleventh-grade exams."

"Uh oh."

"You better ask the teacher if he has an extra book he can sell you to study on your own."

One afternoon several weeks later, Mr. Wright stepped out of the store for a few minutes, leaving Bob in charge of both counters. The bell above the door tinkled, telling him one more person had entered. Since Bob was in the process of ringing up the sale of a customer, he didn't look up but just called out, "I'll be with you in a minute."

"I'll wait," the newcomer said.

I know that voice, Bob thought. Startled, he looked up. Standing at the other end of the counter was his brother, Will.

Another customer came to the register to pay. Without speaking to his brother, Bob took care of that one too.

"Hello, Will," he said after both customers left. "Long time, no see."

"How are you doing, Allister?" Will asked.

Bob winced at being called Allister once more. "Very well, as you can see," Bob answered as levelly as he could.

"How are the studies going?"

"Difficult, but great. Should be graduating from high school the end of June."

"Hope you do, Allister. Have year-end exams to do yet?"

"Yes, of course."

"Think you will pass, do you?"

"Absolutely!"

"Sound pretty sure of yourself."

Bob didn't respond. Will was still capable of raising his ire. "How may I help you?" he asked, intentionally changing the subject.

"I need some money. Since Mr. Wright's not here, and you're in charge of the till, you'll give me $2.00 from that cash register, won't you?"

Bob gasped. *Will's demand implies stealing from my boss, doesn't it?*

From the first month of school last year, Bob had half expected schoolmates to pressure him the way Will was now. But he'd never imagined such a circumstance would be set up by his own brother. Bob looked across the main floor to make sure there were no customers in the store.

Opening the cash drawer, Bob fingered the one dollar bills. *Taking two would be simple. Mr. Wright would probably never miss them.*

"No!" Bob slammed the drawer shut.

Stepping from behind the counter, he flipped a sign on the door and locked it. "Follow me, Will."

Leading his brother up to his room, Bob invited Will to have a seat.

"Saved a little money from my last payday." Bob shook some money from one of Mother's canning jars onto the table in front of Will. "You're welcome to the $2.00 from my own money."

"Thank you, Allister."

Back downstairs, Bob unlocked the front door of the drugstore to let his brother out.

"Will, everyone in Cherry Creek calls me Bob. I'd appreciate it if you did too."

Will's eyebrows went up. "Humph! Well, pay you back in a couple of weeks."

Maybe, Bob thought. *I won't count on it.* He turned the sign on the door. "Be good if you could. See you."

As he watched Will cross the street to his wagon, Bob let out a long breath and revisited what had just happened. *Several years ago, I would have done anything to please this particular brother, to gain his approval. But today I put God's standards for right living and my boss' trust in me ahead of my need for Will's favourable opinion. I had the courage, at last, to do what was right. I didn't give in to the temptation to something wrong just to please my brother.*

Once again, Bob thought about the Bible verse Sam Pollack had shown him during harvest several years ago. *"But seek ye first the kingdom of God, and his righteousness; and all these things shall be added unto you."*[16] Bob realized he had acted for the first time as if he really believed God would keep the promise in the verse.

———◆———

Two weeks later, Will kept his word to pay Bob back. "Thank you for the loan."

"You're welcome."

"Write me when you know if you're graduating."

This brother always has to put in some kind of derogatory dig. Bob bit his lip before responding. "Alright, I will."

Thinking over the exchange later, Bob felt his level of frustration with Will rise once again. *Hmm. No Allis, no Allister, no Bob, either. Now I'm no name. Is there any hope of my brother ever changing his attitude towards me? Are we McRuers a bunch of hard heads? More to the point, do certain men in my family have hearts like the stone from the mountain beyond their farms?*

chapter twenty-four

Twofold Triumph

With the weather warming and the return of the migratory birds overhead, Bob was glad to have some time to play baseball. This was the team's first year together. Swings, misses, strike outs, dropped balls, overthrown bases, and being tagged out seemed to plague their play—so much so, the team from Ninga beat them easily.

"It's alright. It was your first game, after all," their coach said. "Just have some fun."

But when Whitewater beat them too, it didn't exactly feel like fun to Bob. *Oh well, I'm not preparing to be a professional baseball player*, he thought, *but I do aim to become professional at something else.*

———•———

The ominous anxiety over his eleventh-grade exams grabbed and held Bob's focus for weeks before their arrival. *Have I studied hard enough? Do I understand everything sufficiently? Have I outguessed the test writers?*

There were three days of exams this year: Thursday and Friday of one week, a short break for the ninth and tenth graders' exams, and then Wednesday of the next week. Bob's science, math, and drawing tests were on the last day. He hoped the extra hours to review Saturday evening and all day Monday and Tuesday would be the boost he needed. But who could he study with this year? Although Russel had taken the eleventh-grade drawing class and could help Bob study for that subject's exam, neither Russel nor William had taken any of Bob's most difficult science courses. Bob had to do much of his review on his own.

———◆———

"Well, Bob, you did it again," Russell said, looking over his friend's shoulder at the report paper on the desk in front of him.

Bob smiled at his friend. "How did you do?"

"Alright, on the ones I know about. Don't know the results of my second try on the history of Canada exam. They'll post those next week."

"Guess the teachers had to have the eleventh graders' marks ready first so that we'd know if we've graduated or not."

———◆———

Sunday afternoon's graduation ceremony proved to be a scorcher! A small wooden stage sat on top of the pitcher's mound of the ball diamond, facing the outfield. Chairs from classrooms and Cherry Creek's new city hall rested in rows on patches of grass and dirt. Ten minutes before the ceremony was to begin, there was standing room only for parents, siblings, friends, and Cherry Creek School classmates.

Dressed in his best white shirt, vest, coat, and pants, Bob walked with his ten classmates up the central aisle past his whole family, including Will. Since Bob was the only member of his family to graduate from high school, he was sure it was a proud moment for all of them. When all the graduates had received their diplomas, Pa, Mother, John, Will, Mary, Joe, Dan, Jim, and Jessie gathered around to look at Bob's.

"Pretty fancy!" Pa exclaimed. "How much did that piece of paper cost you?"

"Five dollars and years of study."

Some of the tenth graders served lemonade and cake from tables along the first base line. Reverend and Mrs. Wood, Dr. and Mrs. Shaffner, and Mr. and Mrs. Wright came over to congratulate Bob and meet his family.

Russell came over with a man and a woman following him.

"Mother, I'd like you to meet my best friend, Russell," Bob said, before introducing the rest of his whole family.

When it was Russell's turn, he introduced his mother first, then added, "And this is my father, Peter McKinnon."

Bob broke into the widest grin. "Jim, come here! Do you recognize this man?"

"Yep. He's the one who had such a terrible accident our first day in Cherry Creek."

"The red-headed twins!" Peter exclaimed. "Russell, they're the boys who saved my life nine years ago! Thank you, Bob, Jim, thank you! I never got to thank you!"

"You're welcome!" Bob and Jim chimed together.

"Russ," Bob whispered into his friend's ear, "your father's the reason I want to be a doctor."

"Oh!" Russell said, clapping his hand briefly over his mouth. "How long have you suspected my father was the same man?"

"Since the first dinner break during our ninth-grade exams, when our classmate William introduced you to me."

"So that's why you tried so hard to help me! Why didn't you say something?"

"I wanted to be sure," Bob said, smiling.

"Allister, what is Mr. McKinnon talking about?" Father asked.

Russell's father overheard the question and interrupted. "Is it alright if I tell the story, boys?"

"Sure." Bob grinned at Jim. "Go ahead, Mr. McKinnon."

"It all started with a spooked Percheron stallion crashing into my wagon. The hitch broke and my horses ran off. For several long minutes, I lay under my smashed wagon. The weight on top of me crushed my chest. I was in so much pain, I thought I was going to die. I heard many voices. All at once, the weight came off me and I saw many hands lift the wagon up. This young man dragged me out from under it." Mr. McKinnon put his hand on Bob's shoulder.

"He didn't stop there. He asked me questions about my leg. I realized then I couldn't move it. I thought, *It must be broken.* I had no idea how badly damaged it was. But he could see and did the most amazing thing. He wrapped his handkerchief around my leg and, using a stick, twisted the cloth very tight. Hurt like the dickens. He explained he was trying to stop the bleeding.

"More men showed up, put me on a blanket, and carried me to a hotel room. First Mr. Wright came to help me and eventually Dr. Shaffner came. He said my leg had a compound bone fracture. The broken bone had punctured the main vein in my leg. He also said that if your twins hadn't done what they did, I would have bled to death before he got back to town. Dr. Shaffner said your boys saved my life."

When Mr. McKinnon finished the story, Father's mouth hung open and Mother beamed at Bob and Jim. "Thanks for telling us, Mr. McKinnon. Our sons never told us the whole story," she said.

———————

After the Woods, Shaffners, Wrights, McKinnons, and most of Bob's family left, Will asked to spend the night with him. The next day was the Dominion Day holiday celebration, and Will wanted to stay in town for it.

In spite of the avalanche of apprehension his brother's request prompted, Bob agreed. He was totally unprepared for what happened next.

"I need to confess something to you," Will said after they had shared supper in Bob's room. "I've intentionally hurt you over and over. I've teased, taunted, and made your life miserable … because I've always been jealous of you, your abilities, and your brains."

Stunned by Will's confession, Bob shifted in his chair, tears welling from where he had stuffed them long ago.

"I even tried to trick you," Will admitted, "into being less than honest with your job. If you'd done what I asked you to do in Wright's Drugstore a month ago, I could've been responsible for getting you fired. That was wrong, and I'm *so* sorry. You have more integrity in your little finger than I have in my whole body. I know I don't deserve it, but I've stayed to ask you to forgive me. Bob, will you forgive me?"

There was a very long pause.

Bob thought about a phrase he'd just read in his Bible that week: "... *even as Christ forgave you, so also do ye.*"[17] He gulped. Here was a paramount opportunity for his faith to wear shoes in front of Will.

"Yes, Will. I do," Bob said solemnly.

"Thank you." Will stared out the window at a lone boxcar that rested on the track next to the depot across the street.

Bob's eyes followed Will's stare to the boxcar. *Looks just like the one we rode in to Cherry Creek a little over nine years ago.*

"What are your plans now, Bob? Get your own farm? Run a store?"

Bob hesitated answering. *Dare I trust my dreams to this brother of all my brothers? If I never succeed in reaching my goal, will such a failure provide him with an excuse for returning to tormenting me?*

Finally, Bob said, "I want to be a doctor. My next step should be medical school."

Will gasped. "Good grief, that's going to be harder than starting a homestead claim from scratch. Even more than me, you love to pick the hardest thing to do, don't you?"

"Maybe, but I believe I can do it." Bob folded his arms across his chest.

"Hmm. Probably can, at that. But how are you going to pay for it?"

"I will need help," Bob admitted. "I plan to ask Pa."

Will harrumphed. "Pa, is it? When did you start calling Father 'Pa'?"

"There seemed to be a little thaw in our relationship when I turned eighteen." Bob pulled out the pocket watch. "Pa gave me his watch on my birthday."

"Even then, I don't know," Will said, chewing on his mustache. "He can be like ..."

"I know ... a piece of stone. I'm hoping that's no longer the case. I'm praying that Pa will support my reach for my future, just like he has John's, Dan's, and yours."

———•———

Will's two-day visit went more peaceably than Bob could ever have imagined. Will even went with him to watch Bob's team play Ninga during the Dominion Day festivities.

"What position were you playing?" Will asked afterward.

"Shortstop."

"Too bad you fellas lost."

"Yes, it's our third loss out of three games. But the first time we played Ninga, they won by a much bigger margin."

"Improving then?"

"Think so. The team will do better next year, but I won't be with them to help do it. Fun, anyway. Glad I got to play. Had to rearrange my work schedule to participate."

"Mr. Wright's been a good boss then?"

"Absolutely. The best. Been real good to me."

———

Before he left Cherry Creek to return to his homestead claim, Will said, "Let me know how things turn out. You could always come work for me, you know."

Bob felt his mouth drop open of its own accord in flatfooted surprise. *Wow! I can hardly believe my ears. I never expected such a complete change in Will's attitude. Thank you, Lord.*

Snapping his mouth shut, Bob merely nodded. "Alright. I'll keep your offer in mind. Thanks."

———

When Jim came to Cherry Creek in Father's wagon on Tuesday afternoon to move him home, Bob knew he couldn't put off any longer his most difficult goodbye— taking leave of Mr. Wright and his drugstore. "Thank you for trusting me—a complete stranger. The knowledge you shared with me and the encouragement you gave me has meant more than I could ever tell you."

"You're welcome, young Bob. What now?"

"Go home. Help my father, John, Dan, and Jim on their farms this summer. I plan to ask my father for help with medical school. If he agrees, I'll start this fall. Maybe my hope for his help is a pipe dream. He wasn't at all willing to help me with high school. My mother and brothers were the ones who actually did. If my father refuses to help me pay for medical school, I doubt I'll be able to continue my schooling."

"Let me know what happens."

chapter twenty-five

Rebuffed Again

B ob didn't have long to wait for the most difficult conversation of his life to take place. The very next morning, after chores and breakfast, his father set aside the newspaper he had been reading at the kitchen table, put down his cup of tea, and told Bob he wanted to talk to him.

"Son, your mother and I are very proud of you. You are the first one in our family to graduate from high school! Jim showed me your marks. You did well with some difficult subjects, although I don't understand why you took some of the ones you did. At twenty, you are old enough to start your own farm. Jim's getting this section when I get too old to work it, but you could have the eastern half, 320 acres, if you want it. Or I could help you get another piece you like better."

"Pa, I *don't* want to farm!"

Bob watched the muscles in his father's face tighten.

"What do you want to do then?"

"Be a doctor."

"A what?"

"A doctor."

Since his father sat there, saying nothing, Bob continued, "I have taken every math and science course I could. I have even started learning Latin. I have done my best to prepare myself for medical school."

When his father still didn't say anything, Bob added, "You must have known. This can't be a complete surprise. All those medical books I read last summer ..."

Still his father didn't say a word. The man's bushy, salt and pepper eyebrows seemed to move lower into a deeper frown each time Bob looked up.

"Pa?"

"Yes, son?"

"If I wanted to farm like my brothers, you'd do everything to help me. You would assist in locating property and constructing buildings. You would probably loan me livestock and equipment, maybe buy or give me what you could to help me get started. How is helping me with the cost of medical school any different?"

Father slammed his hands down on the table and stood to his full height. "No! No! No! Can't help you!" He shouted and stomped out, slamming the back door behind him.

Stunned, Bob sat for a long time, not moving. It'd taken him nine years and two months to get to this point. Leaning his elbows on the table, Bob put his face in his hands. *I'll never be able to go to medical school. My dream is dead.* Once again, it seemed as if a big zero took the place where his future should be.

Bob felt his mother's hands rest gently on his shoulders. He heard her whispering a prayer over him. Minutes passed. "Ask God to show you what to do," she finally said.

Rising from the bench, Bob blinked back tears of disappointment as he hugged her. Then he went upstairs to sit at his homemade desk that now stood under a window in the bedroom he once again shared with Jim and John. After reading his Bible awhile, he prayed. "Father God, You alone are in charge of my future. That has always been true and is even more obvious to me now. Help me to trust You with it. Please show me what to do and give me the patience to wait until You do."

chapter twenty-six

Puzzle Pieces

A t the noon meal the same day, Bob was given a small piece of an answer to his morning prayer. While they were eating, John talked at length about a girl who was staying with her parents near Desford.

"Addie has caught my eye, and now I'm in a bigger hurry to get my house built," John admitted. "Allister, I could really use your help."

Allister? John called me Allister. Come to think of it, I haven't had a chance yet to talk to him about calling me Bob. Maybe today …

"Come over to my place this afternoon." John headed for the back door. "I'll show you what I have in mind."

"Alright, John."

Dressed in a borrowed pair of his twin's overalls and work boots, Bob walked to his oldest brother's property. Piles of rock lay everywhere. Hitched to a wagon, John's team of Clydesdales stood with heads drooping as they napped in the hot sun.

"Hop on," John said. "I've got a lot more pieces of quarried stone to haul."

When they reached Turtle Mountain's forest, its leaves rustled in a light breeze and filtered some of the intensity of the July heat.

Bob gaped in complete surprise at the quantity of green growth. "A year after the forest fire, wild raspberry bushes overran this part of Turtle Mountain. But now look at it. Stands of poplar and clumps of birch trees. So quickly."

"Turtle Mountain has surprised me too," John said. "I wondered if the forest would ever recover. But it has. In two or three more years, we can start cutting wood for poles, fence posts, and firewood again."

All afternoon John and Bob worked together. After removing the end of the wagon, they shoved pieces of granite boulders up a ramp into the wagon bed. With each haul down the mountain, the piles of rock on John's homestead grew.

"Good thing these trips are downhill," John said. "Easier on my horses."

During a water break, John asked Bob about his last year of school. He wanted to know all about the subjects Bob studied, the work at Wright's Drugstore, the Cherry Creek High School baseball team, and his friend Russell.

"I hear he has a girlfriend," John said as they made a return trip to the mountain.

Bob was amused. A girl was the last thing John usually showed any interest in. At least, that had been true until now. *Hmm. Maybe the girl in Desford has captured more than my brother's eye.*

"Russell's girlfriend is a blonde and blue-eyed wisp of a girl," Bob said. "She's as tall as Russ and a real sweet young lady. A couple of years younger than he. After the Dominion Day ballgame, I asked Russ what his plans were. He told me he'd work on his father's farm for a couple of years before making any other decisions. He wants to give Gwen time to graduate from high school."

"Smart man. How about you? I saw some pretty girls at your graduation."

"Can't, John. I made up my mind a long time ago to finish my education first."

"I thought you had finished."

"No, I haven't. I want to be a doctor. I would need medical college for that."

John let out a low whistle. "Wondered why you took all those math and science classes... and Latin!"

"Big problem isn't the studies. I can handle them. It's money. Father told me this morning he can't help me pay for medical college."

"Thought there was a big blow up. Wondered what it was about. Allister, in recent years you've handled every delay and detour with patience and perseverance. Let this be no exception. What I'll do is hire you to help me build my house. You'll still need to help with chores at home. There will be harvesting to do at Father's, Dan's, perhaps Will's, and mine. But all the other weeks you're available, I'll pay you two dollars a week. Just don't tell anybody else in the family about our agreement. Alright?"

"Absolutely. Sounds great, and thanks. Could I ask you to do me one more favour?"

"Sure."

"Call me Bob, not Allister. The folks in Cherry Creek know me as Robert or Bob. I got used to it."

"Alright, Bob. It's time you left Allis behind. Will stopped calling you that yet?"

"Yes, finally!"

"Good! My little brother has grown up!"

———◆———

When Bob had the opportunity the first week at home, he wrote and posted several letters. His first was to Reverend Wood. There hadn't been time before he left town, but Bob knew he owed his friend a tremendous debt of gratitude for his listening ear, his prayers, and all the wisdom and books the vicar had lent him over the years.

Bob also wrote Russell, Will, and Mr. Wright. Being impatient to receive replies from the latter two, Bob had to find a better way than a nine mile round-trip walk to check the family postbox in the general store at Desford. *I don't want to wait an entire week for someone to check our postbox, and I don't have the time it would take to walk the distance every couple of days.*

While he helped his mother with her horse and buggy after her weekly trip to the Desford store, Bob thought to ask, "Mother, would it be alright if I borrowed Shalazar every other day?"

"I guess so. Why?"

"I'm expecting a couple of important letters. Need to check our postbox. Don't want to wait a whole week."

His mother laughed. "Alright, son."

"Thanks, Mother."

As Bob led the horse to the pasture, he muttered, "Better ask Jim if I can borrow his saddle. Shalazar, riding you will be quicker than harnessing and hitching you up to Mother's buggy."

Shalazar flicked his ears and nodded.

———◆———

The hard physical labour of farm and construction work provided Bob with a break he didn't know he needed. The last two years had been more of a mental workout than he'd realized. With his muscles engaged, his brain had more time and energy to assess what he'd learned, what was important, and what wasn't. It also gave him time to mull over Jack Wright's reply letter when it finally arrived in the family's Desford postbox. *Taking him up on his offer to help me get a pharmacist's apprenticeship license and contract means going an entirely different direction. Change my goal? Is this profession the one You really want me to do, Lord? I've spent years getting ready for medical college. I hate the idea of giving up on my dream!*

Week by week, Bob had the satisfaction of seeing the walls of John's house rise foot by foot. Under Father's tutelage, John had become an able stonemason. Sometimes John, sometimes Father or Dan, would substitute a piece or show Bob how to chisel a rock to make it fit better. The whole goal was to create a thick wall with an almost flat surface inside and out. Getting a similar effect along the edges of open spaces for windows and doors proved to be even more of a challenge.

Since John's house was to be a two-storey building, the height of the wall meant learning to set and mortar stone from wooden scaffolding. Bob was grateful now for the weeks of bricklaying he'd done several years earlier when he and Jim had helped their father put brick siding on the family's farmhouse. That turned out to be a practice run for the stonemason work.

Several times during the summer and fall, the construction of John's house had to be put on hold for other farm work. Late July, there was haying and oat binding and stooking to do. Late August and early September, Pa, Jim, Dan, and John needed help with their wheat and millet harvests.

The middle of September, Bob laid a bundle of his things on top of a small crate of supplies his mother had given him, hoisted the crate onto his shoulder, and headed on foot for Desford. There he begged a ride on a freight wagon returning to Cherry Creek and on another wagon heading north of town along the main road running past Will's farm. Bob's reason for this trip? He had accepted Will's offer for a couple of weeks of harvest work.

Balancing the crate on one shoulder, Bob marched up the lane to Will's farmyard. *I wonder what changes my brother has made to his homestead in the last couple of years. Hmm. Will has extended his pasture fence. Good. And put in a windmill and pump house near the barn. There's a smokestack sticking out of the pump house roof. Will must have a small stove inside to prevent winter freeze up.* Bob smiled. *Still worries about winter freeze up.*

Will's shanty was double the size Bob remembered. A rough frame of studs had even been started for a regular two-storey house in front of the shanty. *Well, I see my brother hasn't waited around for the rest of us to do everything for him. What a relief!*

Bob thought about the spring he, Pa, John, and Jim had come out to Will's place to help build the barn, set up pasture fencing, and construct windows and doors to finish Will's shanty. *All the while Pa insisted Jim and I stay to help Will with his homestead, we were losing precious time in school. I remember how frustrated and angry I was, as if it were yesterday! But digging Will's first well in the mud and slush after a late spring snowstorm had to have been the worst.* Thinking about how chilled he'd gotten from spending entire days in wet pants and boots sent shivers up Bob's spine.

"Hope these weeks on Will's farm won't be anything like my previous experience," Bob muttered.

chapter twenty-seven

Finding His Way

Bob knocked on Will's door. A chair scraped inside and the door burst open.

"Come in, Bob." Will smiled and slapped his brother on the back. "Been expecting you. Got supper ready. Put your clothes in the empty drawer of the dresser in the bedroom and wash up at the pump in the kitchen. We'll eat when you're set."

Handing the crate of supplies to Will, Bob took his bundle of things into his brother's bedroom and looked around. There was a dresser with a mirror. A kerosene lamp sat on top of the dresser. Besides the bed, there was nothing else in the room. Still no curtains or rug. *A bachelor den yet,* Bob thought. Smiling to himself, he plopped his bundle in the empty drawer.

Walking across the main section of the shanty, Bob entered the new room. The pump shed that had been attached to the back of the small house was gone. In its place was a large kitchen. "Smells good, Will."

———

At dawn the next day, Bob helped Will do chores, make breakfast, and groom and hitch up two teams of horses. Will had bought an able Clydesdale partner for the magnificent draft horse that Maggie's colt had become. Will's other team was a pair of golden Belgians. Bob drove the Clydesdales as they drew Will's McCormick reaper across his wheat fields. Will followed, pitching the bound sheaves from the ground onto the hay wagon the Belgians were pulling.

"What happened to the shorthorns?" Bob asked at dinner break.

"After they helped me break up the sod for my fields, I retired them. They were getting too old to really work. They proved to be like many old couples, the second one didn't last long after the first died. Buried them side by side under the far corner of the pasture. Couldn't kill and eat them. They were old friends."

"How long have you had the Belgians?"

"About two years."

"You're pitching the wheat straight onto a wagon. Do you thresh from there?"

"Yep. Eliminates the stooking step."

"What if it rains?"

"The stacked wagons fit in the shed. We'll park them there tonight."

"I'm guessing you don't work at the dairy farm anymore. When did you quit your second job?"

"Haven't quite. Boss hired a younger fella to do six days a week and Sunday evenings. I do Saturday evenings and Sunday mornings, so the boy has some time off and can go to church. Well, let's get back to work. I'll drive the reaper. You pitch."

Bob's memory of his struggle to keep up with this older brother was mollified by the afternoon's pitching experience. At almost twenty-one, six feet tall, and in shape from months of stonemason work, he had no trouble matching Will's pace.

Not long into the switch of jobs, however, and without looking to see where Bob actually was, Will snapped. "You are such a snail, Bob. Would you hustle up?"

Bob frowned. *Guess Will hasn't changed, after all. Why's he so upset?*

After clearing his throat, Bob called Will out. "Did you even look before you yelled at me? I'm having no trouble keeping up with you."

Will turned in the reaper's seat to look. "Oh, so you are. Sorry."

"Sharpening you brain hasn't dulled your brawn any, I see," Will commented at supper. "That's good! I used to think because you moved slow you were lazy. Now I see. You get as much work done as I do. But how?"

"I think about what I'm doing. Don't waste my effort. I make every move count."

"Whereas I hurry and often have to retrace my steps, eh?"

Bob grinned. "You finally got it figured out."

Saturday evening came and Will left to do his milking job. While he was gone, Bob reheated one of his mother's canning jars of beef stew and put the kettle on to boil water for tea. As he waited for Will's return, he could feel a lump of anxiety growing in his gut. "Wonder what he will say when I tell Will I'm planning to attend church at Randy's tomorrow morning," Bob muttered to the kettle on the stove.

Pushing his apprehension aside, Bob brought up the subject during supper.

Will's response was a complete surprise. "Harvest's going along fine. Alright, let's take a Sunday break. After milking tomorrow morning, I'll do some hunting in the marshes north of Whitewater Lake. You're on your own for dinner and probably supper. I'll see if I can get a goose."

When Bob climbed the steps to Randy and Rachel's front porch the next morning, no Sheltie greeted him this time. And unlike his visit years ago, Randy's herd of milk cows was nowhere in sight. No bustle in the barn behind the farmhouse. Nothing but quiet. *Hmm. Randy and Rachel still live here, don't they? Will would have known if they had moved, wouldn't he?*

Bob knocked and waited. Footsteps approached the door.

"Allister, while I live and breathe," Randy exclaimed, reaching for Bob's hand and drawing him into the house. "Rachel, look who's here!"

Rachel came from the kitchen, drying her hands on her apron. "Young man, you've sprouted into a giant oak tree."

As she smiled up at him and reached for his hand, Bob couldn't help noticing the smile lines that wreathed her face and the greying of her temples. *Well, of course. It's been seven years since I have seen these two.*

"You've been reading the Word, I see," Randy said, pointing at the well-worn Bible tucked under Bob's arm.

Bob smiled and nodded.

Rachel moved toward the kitchen. "Won't you have a cup of tea with us before the meeting?"

"Since our oldest son and his wife have taken over our herd," Randy said, "they have made it easier for Rachel and me to continue to host our fellowship on Sunday mornings."

Placing a cup of hot tea on the kitchen table in front of Bob, Rachel added, "Do plan to stay for dinner after the meeting. We'd love to have some time to learn how things have gone for you."

"Thank you, I will."

Since this was Bob's second visit to Randy and Rachel's house church, he knew what to expect. With the group's psalter in hand, he was somewhat successful at following the songs sung a cappella.

During the Scripture sharing portion of worship, Bob stood and read aloud one of his favourite passages—"*For I am persuaded, that neither death, nor life, nor angels, nor principalities, nor powers, nor things present, nor things to come, nor height, nor depth, nor any other creature, shall be able to separate us from the love of God, which is in Christ Jesus our Lord.*"[18]

Towards the end of the service, when it was time to pass the bread and the wine, Bob knew that, unlike his previous visit to their house church, he could actually partake in the Plymouth Brethren group's communion this time—all because Sam from Ontario had shown Bob how to receive Jesus into his heart.

After the worship service, Randy and Rachel shared a potluck dinner from tables in their back yard with Bob and others who stayed. When they had finished eating and the others had left, he had an opportunity to tell the couple about Sam Pollack.

"How Sam ended up at our farm, I'll never know," Bob said, "but his interest in me and his question turned my life around."

Randy and Rachel glanced at each other. With a smile, she laid her hand on Randy's arm.

"We have an idea," Randy said. "You said he asked you a question. What question?"

"What do you plan to do with your life?" Bob rested his arms on the table. "I can still remember exactly what Sam asked me, word for word. I remember his expression. And he really listened to my reply.

"We had many conversations after that. It wasn't long before Sam was teaching me with his Bible open in front of us. He explained how I could have Christ's salvation through faith in Him. For the first time, everything made sense. Most important of all, Sam taught me how to invite the Lord Jesus into my life. I did, and nothing has been the same since."

"That's wonderful, Allister," Rachel said.

"You said you don't know how Sam ended up on your father's farm," Randy said. "Rachel and I know how he did. After you came to our house that Easter Sunday, we prayed for you every day. We asked God to send you someone who could explain God's way of salvation."

"We are delighted He answered our prayer in the way He did." Rachel reached across the table and gently touched Bob's arm.

"I remember you talking about school. Were you able to finish Grade 8?" Randy asked.

With excitement in his voice, Bob shared with his friends his accomplishments. Then with a slump in his shoulders, he also described his disappointment in not being able to reach his ultimate goal—getting the education to become a doctor.

"Allister, you don't have to be a doctor for God to use you to help and bless others," Randy said. "If God has allowed that door to close, you can trust Him to open a different door. Remember the Bible passage you read in meeting today? Believe God does love you. He has your best interests in His heart. Maybe God's plan for you isn't doctoring, but doing something else."

"Wait before Him in prayer," Rachel advised. "Listen for what He tells you to do. Then do it without hesitation or fear."

"You sound like my mother," Bob said, grinning at her, and then laughing with the couple.

As they said their goodbyes later, Bob asked the couple to think of him as Robert or Bob, not Allister. "The folks in Cherry Creek took to calling me Robert or Bob, which is my first name. Even Will is calling me Bob now."

"What's Allister then?" Rachel asked.

"My middle name and a family nickname stuck on me way too long."

"Alright," Randy said. "Since you have a spiritual birthday now as well as a physical one, you are a new creature in Christ, according to God's Word. So it's fitting to have a new name too. We'll continue to pray for you, Bob."

"Thanks. I'll do the same for you and your group here."

"Thank you," she said.

The couple stood side by side with an arm tucked around the other's waist while both waved goodbye. The sight would remain in Bob's memory for many years. "Father God," he whispered, "when it's the right time, please give me a marriage like theirs. Help me to wait for Your time and the woman of Your choice."

Back at Will's place, Bob relished the quiet resting over the homestead. He could use some time alone. Lounging in the kitchen, he sipped some hot tea, read his Bible, and reread the letter Jack Wright had sent him in July. Taking out some paper and an envelope he had brought with him, Bob located Will's pen and bottle of ink to write a letter to his pharmacist friend.

September 22, 1901

Dear Jack,

Thank you for your suggestion. I believe it is the best plan for me. The wages I could earn as an assistant on a farm or in a shop in town would never be sufficient to allow me to save enough for medical school.

I'm currently working for my brother, Will. His harvest should be complete in about a week. On my way home the following week, I'll stop by the drugstore so we can talk. I have about another month of stonemasonry to do on John's house before I can pursue other plans.

Sincerely,

Bob McRuer

chapter twenty-eight

From Farm to Pharmacy

"Pa, it's time for me to move back into town," Bob announced one Friday morning in early November.

"How's Angus' house coming? Thought you promised to help him until it was finished."

"Most of the house *is* finished. The walls and roof are done. The beams for the second floor are ready for the planks. The front and back doors are in, too. John says he can do the rest without me. Besides, Jim and Dan say they're both available to help, now that the harvest is in."

"When do you plan to leave?"

"Monday. Jim's already agreed to give me a ride into town."

"What are you going to do in Cherry Creek?'

"Study for the pharmacist's apprentice test. Mr. Wright wrote he can help me get my apprentice license from the Manitoba government office in Winnipeg, if I pass the test."

"I see. Well, then, you'll be completely on your own. After you leave, there will be no more supplies or laundry from home. Makes too much work for your mother and too many trips for Angus or Jim to town."

"I understand, Pa."

Pa is making it as hard for me to leave as he possibly can, Bob thought. *I can only guess as to why.*

Later the same morning, he walked over to John's place. *After I spend two more days on the house, I'll ask John for some of the wages he's promised.* Bob found John in the living room, mixing plaster for the inside walls.

By Saturday afternoon, Bob had helped John plaster the living room walls and set in the window frames.

"Hope the weather holds long enough," Bob said, "for you to get the house closed off before the real winter weather hits."

"Should be alright. Dan and Jim have promised to work with me next week. Thanks for all your help."

"About my pay ..."

"Oh, right. Well, don't have the money now. Need to sell some wheat."

Bob gulped. He'd been counting on these earnings. He couldn't very well show up in Cherry Creek without a dime. He had to pay for the study books Jack and Mr. Cottingham had arranged for him. "Well, alright. But as soon as you can, mail it to me. I'd appreciate it."

"Might be late November. As you pointed out, I'm in a race against the arrival of winter weather to get my house closed off. Trips into Desford or Cherry Creek to sell grain will have to wait."

Glumly, Bob walked home, hung up his coat, and went to the cistern pump to wash for supper. After supper, he put on his coat and boots to go with Jim to do chores in the barn. When they finished, Jim decided to remain in the barn to spend some time with their father's most recent purchase—a pair of Belgian yearling fillies.

During Bob's amble back across the farmyard, he stuffed his hands into his pockets to warm them. *Hmm. What's this?* Inside the back door, he pulled out a piece of paper from one pocket. A $10.00 bill! *I have no idea who put it there. I saw no one come near my coat.*

Thank you, Father God, he thought. *Between this and the supplies Mother will let me take with me, I have enough for the first month in town. Jack has already offered to let me stay in the room above his drugstore again in exchange for cleaning the store and stoking its furnace.*

———— ◆ ————

Sunday morning Bob walked with his family to the worship service at Wood Lake School. Although he enjoyed singing the hymns as his mother led with the pump organ, he had difficulty focusing on Reverend

Forsythe's sermon. An uncertain future clouded his mind and his time with the families he had gotten to know over the years.

After church, many asked questions Bob wasn't sure how to answer. Rumours had spread he was going back to Cherry Creek.

"Hey, Allister, hear you're leaving us again," a boy's voice called.

When Bob turned to see who it was, all he could do was smile. Georgie, once the smallest boy at Wood Lake School, was now a strapping fourteen-year-old.

"Of course. Time for the next step."

"Which is?"

"An apprentice pharmacist."

"It's life-in-town for you, then?"

"Uh-huh. More to do. Baseball games. Concerts. Plays. More people to meet … like pretty girls. Want to come too?"

"We've got some pretty girls here. Besides, I think we'll be farming with more and more machines. Don't want to miss that."

Bob smiled, remembering Georgie's nose pressed up against the glass of the display case in Desford's general store. Even as a small boy, Georgie couldn't seem to get enough of the toy trains and cars. "Still in love with those engines, eh?"

Georgie laughed. "Of course. If my father ever finds one to pull his plow, I'll be the first to drive it."

"I don't doubt it! Well, God bless you, Georgie, and the next time you see me, call me Bob. They do in town."

Georgie wrinkled his nose and scratched his head. "It'll be hard for me not to think of you as Allister. But alright, Bob."

———

Monday morning's departure was delayed a little. Jim insisted they load the wagon with bagged grain to sell in town. Bob perched his belongings on top—a trunk, a desk, a chair, and packing crates of food supplies from Mother's garden and cellar.

"Might as well make this trip worth the haul," Jim said after they had bid Mother, John, and Jessie goodbye.

"Jim, where did Father go?" Bob asked. "He didn't give me a chance to say goodbye to him."

"He doesn't want you to go!"

Bob sucked in his breath and let it out slowly. *Thought so.*

Jim added, "I think he hoped your graduation from high school would be the end of you leaving."

"How could that be true when all I have ever wanted to be was a doctor?"

Jim reined in Jake and Maggie. He sat, studying his twin, his face registering disbelief.

"I thought you knew," Bob said.

"When did you decide you wanted to become a doctor?"

"When I was fourteen."

"But you never told *me!*"

"I was afraid you'd laugh at me, tell me I could never do it. Like the time you told me I could never go to high school."

"Well, are you?"

"Am I what?"

"Going to be a doctor?"

"Can't. No money to go to medical school. With the wages I can earn now, I'll never have enough money saved for it."

"So that's why the pharmacist's apprentice?"

"Uh huh."

"Will you be doing your apprenticeship in Cherry Creek at Mr. Wright's?"

"No. He says he doesn't have enough traffic to properly train an apprentice."

"Where then?"

"Not sure."

"Mother and Father know you won't be staying in Cherry Creek?"

"No. Please don't say anything about this additional move just yet. I'll let you all know when I have more specific information."

After his arrival in town, Bob spent a little of his cash on a lamp shade, kerosene, and the six books he needed to study. *Ah! To sit and read, undisturbed,* Bob thought, jokingly. *No longer a fish out of water.*

His mind drifted back to the first fishing trip he and his brothers had taken on the Pembina River near Kilarney. While floating on his back in the water, a dragonfly had landed on his nose, and Jim had called him "Bob, the log."

Laughing, Bob thought, *May the dragonflies of knowledge light on me as I become "Bob the log" once more.*

Digging through his trunk for some warmer clothes one day, he found another $6.00 tucked into a corner. *Father may not be supportive of my dreams or my efforts to reach them,* Bob thought, *but other members of my family apparently are.*

Working on John's house until November hadn't left Bob a lot of time to prepare for the test. Poring over science books day and night for weeks made him blurry-eyed with an aching head and a stiff neck and back. He wished Russell was in town and could run with him. On no set schedule, Bob took breaks at odd times, sometimes when the town of Cherry Creek was sleeping. And now that he was in his room most of the day, he had to get used to the noise and rumble of the train as its daily arrival and departure shook the building in which he was sitting.

At the beginning of December, Bob's nonstop studying came to an end. Keeping his promise to Jack, Bob worked full-time in the pharmacy to help with the extra Christmas-time business. Included in Bob's list of tasks was a new one, shoveling snow from the wooden plank sidewalk that now ran past all the stores along the main street.

Early in December, John mailed some of Bob's wages to him. With a little extra money in his pocket and the supplies in his cupboard dwindling, he looked for an alternative to doing his own cooking and laundry. Mrs. Gilbert, Russell's former landlady, struck a bargain with Bob. He could board at her rooming house for $6.00 a month and she would do some laundry for him every other week for forty cents each time. *Having a hot meal to look forward to is wonderful. Too bad I didn't have the money for board and laundry last year. Would have made life so much easier!*

Since Bob's studies in December were limited to after-business hours, he had difficulty with work. Constantly worried about passing the licensure test, Bob's mind would travel at will to the latest information he had pored over the previous evening, often until midnight.

Bob couldn't seem to focus on the customers or on ensuring the accuracy of the mental math required for making sales. Several times a week Bob had to calculate from written columns of numbers on scraps of brown packaging paper to be certain of charging the correct amount. *Slows up the process. Bad thing to have to do at such a busy time. Didn't need to do this last year. What's the matter with me?* In the middle of his moments of fretting, he would catch himself yawning.

A couple of days before Christmas, the licensure test arrived. Under Jack's watchful eye, Bob sat in the drugstore's back room and worked his way through its pages in a couple of hours. When they were completed, the pharmacist put them in an envelope.

Bob stretched. *What a relief! Glad it's done!*

Jack gave Bob a form to fill out. It was an application for a pharmacist's apprentice license. He looked at the blanks for his name: last name, McRuer; first name, Robert; middle initial A. *If anyone ever asks me what the A stands for*, he thought, *I'll be tempted to answer some name other than Allister.*

"Well, what do you think, Bob?" Jack asked. "How was the test?"

"Much to my surprise, it was easier than any exam I took my last year of high school."

"Good. Here's a dollar for the filing fee and the address to mail the envelope. Do it today!"

"Thank you, Jack."

After addressing the envelope, Bob headed down the street to the post office. *Well, Father God, once again, my future is in Your hands. I have done what You have shown me to do. Will I pass?*

Anticipation

B ob worked on Christmas Eve until 4:00 p.m. If he hurried, he could catch a ride with the last freight driver to Desford. When Bob climbed into the wagon, the driver waved an envelope under his nose. "Postal clerk gave me this to give to you," the man said.

"Thanks." Bob glanced at the postmark. *Elgin. Could it be from Will?*

Bob tore the end open and pulled out two bills, a $10 and a $5, and a note.

December 17, 1901
Dear Bob,
　　Here's something to help your quest. Happy 21st birthday and Merry Christmas.
Sincerely, Willie

Bob sat silently with tears springing into the corners of his eyes. After reading the note several times, he stuffed the envelope with its contents into his pocket and brushed his eyes with the back of his hand.

"Who's Willie?" the driver asked.

"One of my older brothers."

"Good brother."

"Yes, he's become one recently."

"Why do you say that? What did he do before?"

Bob recalled several incidents of Will's mean-spirited name-calling and derogatory comments.

"Looks like he's said he's sorry."

"Yes, sir, I guess he has!"

Mother was dishing up Christmas Eve supper when Bob walked in the door. Jessie and Tawny tackled him before he got too far. "Merry Christmas, Allister."

"Merry Christmas to you too, sis … Tawny …" Bob leaned over to pat the Sheltie. *I'll probably never be able to get Father or Jessie to call me by my preferred name,* he thought with a sigh.

"Glad you could make it, son," Mother said. "Mary and Joe, John and John's Mary, and Dan will be here tomorrow for Christmas dinner."

"John's living at his own place now?"

"Yes, yes. It's so nice!" Jessie exclaimed. "Wait 'til you see it!"

After supper, the only person to open a Christmas Eve present was Jessie. His thirteen-year old sister's eyes sparkled when she opened her gift. Mother had crocheted a pretty, white, lacy collar to go on Jessie's maroon, corduroy Christmas dress from last year. *Jessie is growing so fast right now,* Bob thought, *she won't be able to wear that dress another year. Hope I'm done growing. None of the pants Mother bought me fit me anymore, and a few of the shirts she's made me don't, either. Besides, I need to look more like a professional and less like a farmer. I'll have to use a fair amount of my cash just for clothes. I saw shirts with detachable collars for seventy-five cents, and a suit at Nicol's Store for $14.00. Maybe after Christmas …*

With at least some form of a future taking shape, Bob could relax enough to really enjoy the most important holiday of the year with his family. The candlelight Christmas Eve service was always simple yet beautiful with its carols, Scripture lessons, and a candlelit carol outdoors at the end. *Will I even be able to come home for any future holidays? Or will I be alone in some strange town next Christmas?*

Christmas morning was always exciting, even if Jessie was the only child still in the house. Her excitement bubbled over to everyone. After breakfast, chores, and gifts for those still at home, Mother bustled about the kitchen, ordering Jim, Bob, and Jessie about. For some reason, she wanted everything to be especially perfect this year.

As the family gathered around the dining room table for Christmas dinner, Jessie was full of chatter as usual. "Allister," Jessie piped, "John has a girlfriend. See?"

"Hello," the young woman said to Bob as she squeezed into the chair between him and John. "John tells me to call you Bob. My name is Mary Adelaide. Just call me Addie."

"Glad to meet you, Addie," Bob said, shaking her hand.

At the end of the delicious meal, John interrupted the conversations around the table. "Addie and I are engaged to be married. Earlier today, I asked. She said yes!"

"Congratulations!" everyone said at the same time.

"Have you two set the date yet?" Father asked.

John looked at Addie and then said, "Well, we talked about a June wedding, but we haven't picked an exact date yet."

"Isn't this exciting?" Jessie shouted, clapping her hands. "John, can we show Allister the insides of your new house? Addie, Allister left before John finished it."

"Good idea. Addie hasn't been inside it yet, either," John said. "Who else wants a tour? Follow me."

Everyone marched through the snow to John's house on the next homestead claim. Stomping the snow from their boots on the porch at the front door, the whole family entered and wandered about John's stone house, upstairs and down.

"John, you did a beautiful job of finishing the house," Bob said. He then turned to John's fiancée. "Well, what do you think, Addie?"

"It's wonderful, Bob. Jessie's already told me you helped build it. I think she called the walls of this house its 'outsides.'"

Bob laughed. "John quarried most of the stone for this house from Turtle Mountain. And I helped build its outsides, like Jessie says. Dan and Joe helped finish its insides after I left for Cherry Creek."

"Bob, thanks for your part in what will be John's and my home." Addie took John's hand. "I can hardly wait for the day I'll share it with you."

"We've a little time before we get married, Addie. You can help me select a better cooking range from the *Sears, Roebuck* catalogue. Then we need …"

Bob wandered off, leaving the couple to their homemaking plans. *Wonder how long I will have to wait to get married. Hope my wait won't be as long as John's. He's almost thirty-two.*

The afternoon of Boxing Day, the day after Christmas, Bob thanked his mother for the wonderful meals and said goodbye to his family once more. Since it was a national holiday, Bob knew there would be no freight wagons on which to hitch a ride. He walked the twelve miles back to Cherry Creek.

True to his promise, Jack helped Bob get a full-time job in the claims office at the new Central District Hall. The office Bob had visited with Dan and John years ago had moved from Deloraine to Cherry Creek. Now it was Bob's responsibility to check paperwork and maps of claimed sections of land on Manitoba's southwestern prairies. For this office work, he was paid the grand sum of $8.00 per month.

It wasn't long before his new boss asked if Bob would do some overtime. Although the extra money would help Bob save more money, more time at his new job presented a problem.

"Jack, the claims office in District Hall has asked me to work more hours, but that'd mean I wouldn't be available to work at the drugstore. What should I do?" Bob asked one Saturday morning while they waited for the first customer.

"Go ahead. You need the money. Don't worry about my drugstore. I should be able to hire a local boy for the after-school and Saturday morning hours."

"May I still live in the room upstairs, even though I won't be working for you?"

"Certainly. Just earn your room by keeping the furnace stoked and the drugstore's floors clean, like you were before. In reality, you'll still be working for me. I own the building where your claims office is."

"Oh!" Bob exclaimed with a laugh. "I had no idea!"

———

During his dinner hour in late January, Bob thought to check his postal box in the Cherry Creek train depot. A large envelope from Winnipeg was being kept behind the clerk's counter for him.

"Well, Bob, if I dare be so nosey, what did you get in the mail?" the clerk asked.

Bob stared. He was almost afraid to open it.

"Well, go on. The suspense is killing me," the clerk said.

Bob gently tugged on the flap. When it finally yielded, he pulled out a highly scrolled and elaborately printed license for a pharmacist's apprentice.

The clerk whistled. "Good golly. You should have that framed."

"Someday I will. Right now, I'd better show it to Jack."

"Will you be his apprentice?"

"No. He told me he has already written to several other pharmacists in bigger towns."

"Well, good luck. Here's the mail for the drugstore."

While Bob walked back to the store, he flipped through the envelopes. There was one from a Mr. Halpin in Brandon. *Is this the letter that will affect my future?*

chapter thirty

Promises

S everal more months went by. Letters arrived for Mr. Jack Wright from three other places. Still Jack said nothing to Bob about the contents of the letters.

Averaging $3.00 a month in overtime pay, Bob could save some money and still pay for a few extras. He bought a bike for $11.00 to make his visits home easier.

John stopped by. He had sold another load of grain in town and could pay Bob the rest of the wages promised. When John saw a bike leaning against the wall at the bottom of the stairs to the second floor, he said, "I'm guessing the bike is yours, Bob. Know how to ride it?"

"No, not yet."

"Well, don't break your neck trying! Good luck!"

Much like John's warning, Bob wrecked the bike's front wheel the very first time he tried to teach himself to ride. Then all he could do was groan, not so much from the accident as from the cost of straightening the bent wheel. The repair was almost as much as the bike itself. But since those two wheels were his only non-horse transportation, he stuck to it until he mastered the ride.

Other extras he could now pay for were a concert or two, some ice cream, a shave as well as a haircut, and an additional Latin book.

In May, another letter arrived from Brandon. This time Jack shared its contents.

"Bob, a friend of mine runs a drugstore in Brandon and wants to offer you a year's apprenticeship under his supervision. Mr. Halpin's enclosed a contract in this letter. He'd like you to sign it, if you accept his offer. Be sure to read all of its terms first. He also needs to know if you'd like him to make boarding house arrangements for you."

Bob took the contract upstairs to study. If he signed, he was agreeing to be an apprentice for one year at Mr. Halpin's drugstore. Bob's responsibilities would include making prescription medication compounds according to the pharmacist's recipes and processes per doctor's orders. His pay would be $25 a month. If he completed his apprenticeship successfully, he'd be offered a full-time pharmacist position under the head pharmacist. The new position would come with raises in salary. The contract also said that he'd be given two weeks of paid vacation annually.

Bob read and reread the contract. Its terms spelled out more blessings than he'd ever hoped for. *Twenty-five dollars a month! Saving for college should be no problem. Thank You, Father God!*

Bob readily signed with a flourish: Mr. Robert A. McRuer.

When Bob mailed the contract, he included a letter thanking the man for the wonderful opportunity to learn from such an experienced pharmacist. Bob also requested help with finding a reasonably priced boarding place within walking distance of the store.

Before the end of May, Bob received a reply. In Mr. Halpin's letter, Bob learned his starting date and the address of a recommended boarding house in Brandon.

The first week of June, Bob had to set aside his own excitement to plan his part in his brother John's wedding. During several dinner hours, Bob shopped for the right wedding gift.

Turning down overtime the first Saturday of the month, Bob rode his bicycle the twelve miles home. Leaning his wheels against the back of the house, Bob ran upstairs to Jim's bedroom to change from his bike pants to his suit pants. After attaching a collar to his shirt, knotting a tie, combing his hair and mustache, and wiping the dust from his black, polished shoes, he felt ready to usher at his oldest brother's wedding. Jim dashed in just then and hustled into clean clothes. Together the twins walked over to join the rest of the family for the ceremony at Wood Lake School.

The wedding meal and reception was held in John's stone house and on its porch. Addie's mother and her mother's neighbours from Desford took over John's kitchen. There were no scones or a wedding cake made of fruitcake, but the food was delicious and plentiful.

Bob eyed the white wedding cake with its fluffy, scalloped frosting. *Hmm. Not what I expected. But Addie's family isn't Scottish like ours. They probably have different traditions.* With a slice of cake and a cup of tea, Bob joined three of his brothers as they lounged on the porch.

"Alright, Bob, out with it!" Dan demanded.

"Out with what?" Bob asked.

"Your latest plans," Jim said. "You promised you'd let us know when you knew."

"Umm. Alright. I have my license to be an apprentice and a year's contract to work under the supervision of a pharmacist."

"Which one?"

Before Bob could answer, John joined the group. "Yes, which one?" he repeated.

"Mr. Halpin in Brandon."

There was silence while that piece of news sunk in.

"When?" Will finally asked.

"September."

"Until then?"

"Work at District Hall."

"Mother and Father know yet?" John asked.

"No. Haven't had a chance to talk to them. I'll tell them later today."

"Are you still going to try for medical school?" Will asked.

"No. Not medical school. Pharmaceutical college."

"When?" Jim asked.

"Don't know. It'll take some time to save enough money for it."

"Still studying Latin?" John asked.

"Oh yes. Bought one more Latin book to pore through."

"You're a studying fool," Dan finally added.

"A student—of God's Word and other books—I am, absolutely!" Bob had the confidence to come back with, "but I am no fool!"

———◆———

When Bob did tell his parents about his plans, Mother looked sad about how far away he'd be. "You'll write, won't you, son?"

"Of course, Mother."

"Come home for Christmas?"

"Won't be able to. But I'll have vacation time—probably in the summer. I'll come home then."

"Still plan to go to medical college?" Father asked.

"No. Pharmaceutical college."

"Pharma ... what?"

"I plan to go to college to become a full pharmacist. I want to have and run my own drugstore."

"Where's the college?"

"In Winnipeg."

"How'll you pay for it?"

"Work, save money."

"Humph! Bet you can't. Better stick to your job."

Bob frowned. *Pa doesn't believe that I can or that I will.*

———◆———

Summer months sped by. Before he knew it, it was time for Bob to collect his last pay and say goodbye to co-workers at the District Hall, Reverend Wood, Mrs. Gilbert, and Dr. Shaffner.

Bob had promised to spend at least a week at home before he left for Brandon. Since it was the first week in September, he borrowed work clothes from Jim again and for the last time worked with his father and brothers on the harvest.

Ten days later, he rode his bike back alone to Cherry Creek. With the annual threshing in full swing, no one in his family could see him off. Back in town, he collected his packed trunk from Wright's Drugstore. Shaking hands with Jack and saying goodbye at the train depot across the street from the store, Bob paid $3.25 for his ticket, saw his bike and trunk to the freight car, and boarded the train westward bound to Napinka.

Settling into his seat in the passenger car for the first leg of his journey, he thought about the last time he'd been on a train a little more than ten years ago. *Shared a smelly box car with all my father's livestock for two weeks. Endured nonstop taunting from Will.* Bob's stomach tightened. He remembered how angry he'd gotten with Will, how quickly he had lost his temper and taken swings at his brother. *Well, all that is behind me now. Will has changed. He has even apologized for the way he treated me. And the Lord is helping me get a better handle on my spirit.*

This train trip I have a comfortable seat. I'll have a chance for pleasant conversation with other passengers and this ride is a lot shorter—only two days.

The biggest difference is it's my choice to go. This is God's door of opportunity that He has amazingly opened for me. Certainly, I will walk through it. Wonder what's on the other side?

chapter thirty-one

A Is for Arthur

The train clickety-clacked to Whitewater. Then to Deloraine. It no longer returned from that town, but continued through to Napinka. At its last stop, passengers could catch a train travelling west into the province of Saskatchewan or go northeast to Brandon and Winnipeg.

At the junction, Bob got off the train. After seeing to the transfer of his luggage and bicycle to the freight area in the depot, he checked into a recommended boarding house near the depot.

Early the next morning, he caught the train going north. Seven and a half hours and six stops later, Bob stepped off the train into a busy, noisy depot. He followed the luggage cart into the freight office. Writing down the address for the clerk at the desk, he paid twenty-five cents to have his trunk delivered to his boarding house.

Intending to ride his bicycle through town, Bob asked the clerk for directions to the nearest post office and the boarding house. The elderly gentleman rambled through a lengthy list of turns. "Go north two blocks along the street out front, turn ..." The man pointed in different directions while he gave the detailed instructions. He ended his list of turns with, "You can't miss it."

Although Bob only remembered a fraction of the instructions, he got on his bicycle to begin the final segment of his journey. Growing up on a pioneer farm and living for three years in a small town had in no way prepared him for dealing with the traffic of a city. He'd never seen so many horses, wagons, buggies, and people in his life. It was worse than Cherry Creek on Dominion Day! Bob didn't know whether to be afraid or excited. *Maybe both*, he decided.

Trying not to get run over, Bob pedalled with the flow of vehicles until he came to the first intersection. Learning from what the other drivers did, he got across safely.

A block further on, Bob stopped at the post office to buy some stamps. As he rummaged in his pockets for the ten dollars he had left, he discovered three ten-dollar bills! Again someone in his family had snuck him some money. Must have been just before he left home. "Whew!" Now he had enough to cover his expenses until he received his first pay. *Thank you, Lord*, he thought. *Bless that person please, Father God*.

After Bob bought the stamps and some shoe polish in a shop further down the block, he returned to the problem of finding his rooming address. Pedalling around blocks in different directions, he hoped to run into the correct street at least. Not all the streets had signs. At last he admitted he was lost and needed to stop wasting time. The very next person he saw, he asked.

"Oh, not far. One block that way. Turn left. Half a block down. West side of the street."

Thanking the woman, Bob had no trouble finding the house this time.

"Velcome, Bob," Mrs. Van derworts said, greeting him at the door. "You trunk is already here. Vat happened to you? Ve vere beginning to dink ve might need to contact da police to report a missink person."

"Got lost."

"Didn't ask direksuns?"

"Well, yes, ma'am, I did. But I couldn't remember them all and I'm not familiar with the streets here yet. Our town of Cherry Creek is a whole lot smaller than Brandon."

"Vell, no matter, younk man. Let's put you bicycle in da back sed. You trunk is up in you room already. After supper, I take you up dere. Hungry?"

"Starved!"

"All dat bicycle ridink … ya, dat make you hungry, I'm sir."

Alone in his new room after supper, Bob unpacked his trunk. Against the wall opposite the door there was a wardrobe in which to hang his suit and shirts. To the right of the door stood a chair and a small table with a lamp under the one curtained window overlooking a postage stamp-sized front yard and the street. To the left of the door was a wash stand. Between the stand and the bed was a dresser in which to put the rest of his clothes. A single iron bedstead with fresh linens and a handmade quilt lined the adjacent wall. Next to the bed on the floor lay a colourful, braided rug. Bob slid the trunk on the rug until he had the big box at the foot of his bed. Then he put his stack of books on the table.

Lighting the lamp, he sat and opened his Bible to do his usual bed-time reading. Having read all way through the New Testament several times in the last two years, Bob had started to read through the Old Testament. During the train ride, he had read in the book of Joshua about God flattening the walls of Jericho for His people when they obeyed Him. Bob looked at the first sentence of each of several chapters. "*And it came to pass…. Now it came to pass…*"[19] he read over and over. Bob threw his head back, roaring in hilarious relief and almost disbelief. He knew from the context the phrase, "it came to pass," meant "it happened that …" But he thought about another meaning for the same phrase. "It came to pass," Bob read aloud softly again, adding, "and not to stay! No circumstance continues forever. Thank you, Heavenly Father, for helping me to understand!"

Even in his strange surroundings, Bob realized he was perfectly at peace with his situation and future. True, the door to medical school was closed to him. Also true, he didn't know exactly what lay ahead. But he sensed he was in God's place for him at God's time. His Lord would continue to guide him, but he needed to listen to and follow directions. Bob's experience of getting lost that afternoon had reinforced the point!

When Bob slid between the sweet-smelling, clean, pressed sheets that night, he felt as if he had landed in the lap of luxury. *No more scratchy, wool blankets against my chin.*

Since Bob had arrived in Brandon on Friday afternoon, he had two days to rest, get acquainted with the family with whom he was boarding, and acclimate himself to the streets of the city. Within forty-eight hours, he knew which directions from his boarding house were north, east, south, and west. He learned how to get to the post office, the closest Presbyterian church, and Halpin's Drugstore.

Sunday evening, Bob took out a couple of pieces of paper, a pen, and an ink bottle. Turning to the book of Matthew in his Bible, he wrote out the verse that Sam Pollack had shown him all those years ago. "*But seek ye first the kingdom of God, and His righteousness; and all these things shall be added unto you.*"[20] Bob folded the paper and set it in a conspicuous spot on the table. *I think I will need this reminder to keep my priorities straight in the days to come.*

Bob took out a second piece of paper and an envelope. *Now it's time for me to keep my promise to Mother.*

Brandon, Manitoba
September 14, 1902
Dear Mother,
I arrived safely on the afternoon of the 12th. My room is very pleasant, and the Van derworts take good care of their boarders. The Mrs. is a very good cook, but not as good as you, of course. No scones. Lots of cheese. The only problem is the price—$4.50 per week. I hope to find a cheaper place to board soon.

I've already decided to sell my bicycle. The traffic here is horrendous.

I found the two ten dollar bills. Say a thank you to whoever must have put them in my pocket just before I left home.

Tomorrow, I start work. Please continue to pray for me.
Much love, Bob

Up early Monday and dressed, Bob checked his appearance in the full-length mirror on his wardrobe door. He straightened his narrow, stiff, white collar and black tie. Reaching up the sleeve of his black suit, he tugged at one of the cufflinks on the cuff of his pressed white shirt. He lifted one shoe and then the other to check how well the black socks matched the polish with which he had shined his shoes.

No longer a light, fiery red, his hair had grown out a deep auburn this past year. Now its short, wavy top lengths were parted in the middle and slicked down. His lighter auburn mustache had been trimmed and brushed.

I look more like a modern pharmacist than a farm boy now, he thought with satisfaction.

Bob ran downstairs and made short work of breakfast when Mrs. Van derworts brought it to the dining room. "Gut luck!" she called as he headed for the door.

———

As Bob walked down the block towards the drugstore, he passed a building under construction. He turned back to watch the bricklayers as they scurried up scaffolding. *I may be only twenty-one,* Bob thought, *but I've done enough building projects to last me a lifetime!*

Arriving before the drugstore's usual business hours, Bob found its front door locked. He knocked. While he waited for someone to answer, he checked his hair, collar, and tie in the reflection of the door's window. *Guess I am a little nervous. Understandable. It is my first day in a totally new situation with a new boss.*

When a young man opened the door, Bob said, "Hello, sir. I am Robert McRuer. I believe you are expecting me?"

"Yes, we are. Come in. I am Grant Cowper, Mr. Halpin's business partner."

"I'm glad to meet you, Mr. Cowper. Please call me Bob."

"Alright, Bob. Mr. Halpin is in the back office. Please follow me."

As he crossed the drugstore's main floor, Bob looked around. *Hmm. A lot more inventory to keep track of. Some items I've never seen before. Well, I am here to learn.*

Mr. Halpin met Bob at the door to the office. "Welcome, Robert." He shook Bob's hand. "You've met Grant. Before we open the store, I would like you to sign and date this time sheet. You can sit here at my desk while you do it."

Mr. Halpin leaned over Bob's shoulder while he signed in. "Robert A. McRuer," the pharmacist read aloud. "Just like you signed your contract. I am a little curious. What does the A stand for?"

"Allister," Bob mumbled with his back to his new boss because he was still writing.

"Arthur?" Mr. Halpin asked, cupping his hand over his ear. "Did you say Arthur?"

Turning towards Mr. Halpin, Bob said, "Yes, sir, you guessed correctly. The A means Arthur. Sorry, I'll speak up from now on."

As Mr. Halpin began the numerous instructions Bob would receive over the next few months, he realized he was finally rid of the farm boy who had wrestled for a decade with the name Allis. He was now Robert Arthur McRuer, an apprentice pharmacist—with no farm, but full of hope for a great future.

Epilogue

A major calamity threatened Bob's future when Mr. Halpin died of typhoid fever two months after Bob started his apprenticeship. Through a provision in Mr. Halpin's will, Bob completed his apprenticeship, receiving his pay from Mr. Halpin's estate.

It took Bob two additional years of working at Halpin's Drugstore (with occasional raises in pay) to save up enough money to go to the College of Pharmacy in Winnipeg. He had successfully completed the first semester of his pharmaceutical classes before his father finally relented and agreed to help Bob with expenses for his final semester of courses. In May of 1906, Bob graduated as Mr. Robert Arthur McRuer, Pharmacist.

Shortly after graduation, Bob was put in charge of a startup pharmacy in St. Boniface, Manitoba, partly because he could speak French. With his father assisting him financially once again, Bob bought the inventory for that pharmacy business in November, 1906. Bob's Pa had finally seen what his son could do and in the end did help him.

During the first year of running his own store, Bob studied optometry. Within a year, he had added Dr. Robert Arthur McRuer, Optometrist, to his ability to serve his new French-speaking community.

Bob married, had four children, which included a set of twins, and spent over fifty years helping to heal bodies, assist eyes with better sight, and encourage those who would listen to meet and follow his Saviour and Lord, Jesus Christ.

End Notes

1. Romans 3:23
2. Romans 6:23
3. Ephesians 2:8–9
4. Titus 1:2
5. Acts 4:12
6. John 3:3
7. John 3:5–6
8. John 3:16–18
9. John 3:36
10. Revelations 3:20
11. I John 5:11–13
12. Matthew 6:33
13. Psalm 3:5
14. Romans 5:3–5
15. Proverbs 16:32
16. Matthew 6:33
17. Colossians 3:13b
18. Romans 8:38–39
19. Joshua 4:1; 5:1; 9:1; 10 1; 11:1
20. Matthew 6:33

Glossary

Allegory—a story with characters who symbolize people in general

Angus—a breed of hornless beef cattle, originally from Scotland. In this series, these cattle are red, not the usual black. Also in this series, Bob's oldest brother is called Angus by their father because that is John's middle name.

Beau—a girlfriend or boyfriend

Belgians—a breed of heavy, muscular horses, often gold in colour with a white mane and tail

Binder (or reaper)—a horse-drawn farm machine that cuts and binds grain crops into sheaves or bundles

Boissevain—modern name for the town of Cherry Creek

Breech birth—the birth of a baby hind end, instead of head, first. When a calf or infant is turned the wrong way inside its mother, she has a difficult time with the delivery of her young.

Clydesdales—a breed of heavy draft horses, originally from Scotland. They are usually deep brown in colour with a black mane and tail and have long, silky hair on their legs.

Commode—a chair holding a chamber pot under an open seat, a toilet

Compound—something made by combining two or more ingredients in definite proportion by weight

Compound fracture—a broken bone such that the bone pieces stick through the skin

Desford—a small town with a general store and a grain elevator. At the time frame of this series, Desford is only four and a half miles from the McRuer homestead and the closest town.

Dump rake—a wheeled horse-drawn farm machine with a row of curved tines. The operator lowers the tines to turn mown grass for better drying and to gather the drying grass (hay) into windrows.

Dodge—a last-minute way to avoid an unwelcome outcome

Epiphany—a sudden understanding of reality through something simple, yet striking

Filly—a young female horse

Gelding—a castrated male horse, no longer a stallion

Heifer—a young cow, one that hasn't yet had a calf

Itinerant—travelling from place to place, usually to do a certain type of work

Kiln—an outdoor, heated enclosure used for processing bricks

Mortar—a mixture of cement, lime, or gypsum plaster with sand and water that will harden after a stonemason uses it to build

Nemesis—a strong opponent who usually wins. In this book, Allister's temper is his nemesis.

Percherons—a breed of powerful draft horses, often dappled gray in colour

Phosphate—a carbonated drink

Pitcher—a farm worker who uses a pitchfork to throw straw or hay onto a wagon or hay rack during harvest

Plymouth Brethren—an evangelical, Protestant, Christian denomination

Proctor—one appointed to supervise students during an examination

Psalter—a collection of psalms or songs for use in worship

Quarry—to cut or dig out stone for building

Rebuffed—rejected

Rhetoric—the study of speaking as a means of persuasion

Sad-iron—a metal household tool that is heated on a stove before being used to smooth wrinkles out of clothing

Scaffold—a temporary platform that workers can stand or sit on while they build above ground level

Scribbler—a bound booklet of lined paper. A student uses it to keep notes or write his or her homework assignments.

Soda jerk—a person who serves carbonated drinks at a soda fountain

Soddy—a house usually made of chunks cut from sod, often with a grassy sod roof. In this book, it is a home started by digging a space into a steep slope.

Squiring—escorting a girl to special places, similar to dating

Stalemate—a deadlocked contest, neither side is winning

Stallion—a male horse, usually kept for breeding

Stonemason—a skilled worker who builds by laying units of stone or brick

Stooking—the action of standing several bound sheaves of drying grain on their butt ends, leaning into each other

Tarpaulin—a piece of heavy, water-shedding fabric used as a temporary shelter

Tome—a large or scholarly book

Toonie—a Shetland Sheepdog or Sheltie, originally from Scotland. These small dogs could be kept in town (toun, hence toonie) or used to herd livestock on farms.

Vouch—to give supporting testimony, to give a guarantee

Windrows—rows of hay raked up to dry before being stored

Wood Lake School—one-room schoolhouse built on the northwest corner acre of the McRuer family homestead. The McRuers and local farmers built the school in 1893. Allister and Jim attended grades seven and eight at this school in 1893–1895.

Photos

ROBERT A. McRUER. WINNIPEG, MB. ~1906.

MCRUER WOOD-FRAME FARMHOUSE WITH BRICK VENEER
AND KITCHEN ADDITION. IT WAS LOCATED NEAR DESFORD, MB,
AND SIX MILES NORTHEAST OF TURTLE MOUNTAIN.

JOHN MCRUER'S STONE HOUSE. BUILT ON HIS HOMESTEAD NEXT TO THE
JAMES MCRUER HOMESTEAD WITH ROBERT MCRUER'S HELP IN 1901.
THE AUTHOR TOOK THIS PHOTO OF THE HOUSE IN 2008.

WOOD LAKE SCHOOL CAIRN. ONE-ROOM SCHOOLHOUSE BUILT ON
THE CORNER ACRE OF THE JAMES McRUER HOMESTEAD IN 1893.

CENTRAL SCHOOL. BUILT IN BOISSEVAIN, MB, IN 1894.

2

Boissevain Sept 30th 1899

Sep 30	To Amt Received				5	00
Oct 3	..	..	..		5	00
29	"	"	"		1	00
Nov 20	"	"	..		5	75

16 | 75

PAGE 2 OF R.A. McRUER'S CASH JOURNAL.

		Sept 189..		**3**
Sept	30	Dish & au		35
"	"	Cap		50
Oct	2	Literature Book		35
"	3	Trunk	3	00
"	"	School Fee	1	00
"	"	Mother's Horse		15
"	"	Bottle Ink		10
"	7	Bread		60
"	"	Sugar		25
"	17	Boots	2	25
"	"	Bread		25
"	21	Bose Sodas		25
"	24	School Literature		25
"	25	Bread		25
"	30	"		25
Nov	11	Coal oil		35
"	11	Bread		25
"	20	Rubbers		50
"	21	Bread		20
"	28	Scribblers & ect.		25
"	"	School Fee	3	00
	"	By Balance	1	85
			16	

PAGE 3 OF R.A. MCRUER'S CASH JOURNAL.

22

		Brought For'd	27	75
Dec	23	To Aunt Ree from Willie	15	00
"	-	To " for Posting B	1	00
- 1902		- - - - - - -		
Jan	4	To moeatery at Wrights	12	00
	6	" Book to Cottingham	1	00
	10	" " " "	5	00

61 75

Dec	~	By Aunt B.T.	13	45
"	9	Shaving Soap		15
"	"	Honey		20
"	11	Pair Pants	3	00
"	~	" Boots	2	00
"	17	1/2 doz Knives	1	25
"	~	Salmon		20
"	~	Bread		25
"	23	Suit of Cloths	14	00
"	~	Haircut!		25
"	27	Baptist C.S.S. Ent.		25
Jan	2	Cash Book		25
"	4	Good from Wrights	1	00
"	4	Shirt		50
"	1	Repairing boots		20
"	6	Mr J.W.S. Board for Dec	3	00
"	6	Shirt & collar		75
"	9	Latin Book	1	00
"	10	Cap		45
"	11	Collars		40
"	11	Laundry		30
		Balance	18	90
			61	95

PAGE 23 OF R.A. McRUER'S CASH JOURNAL.

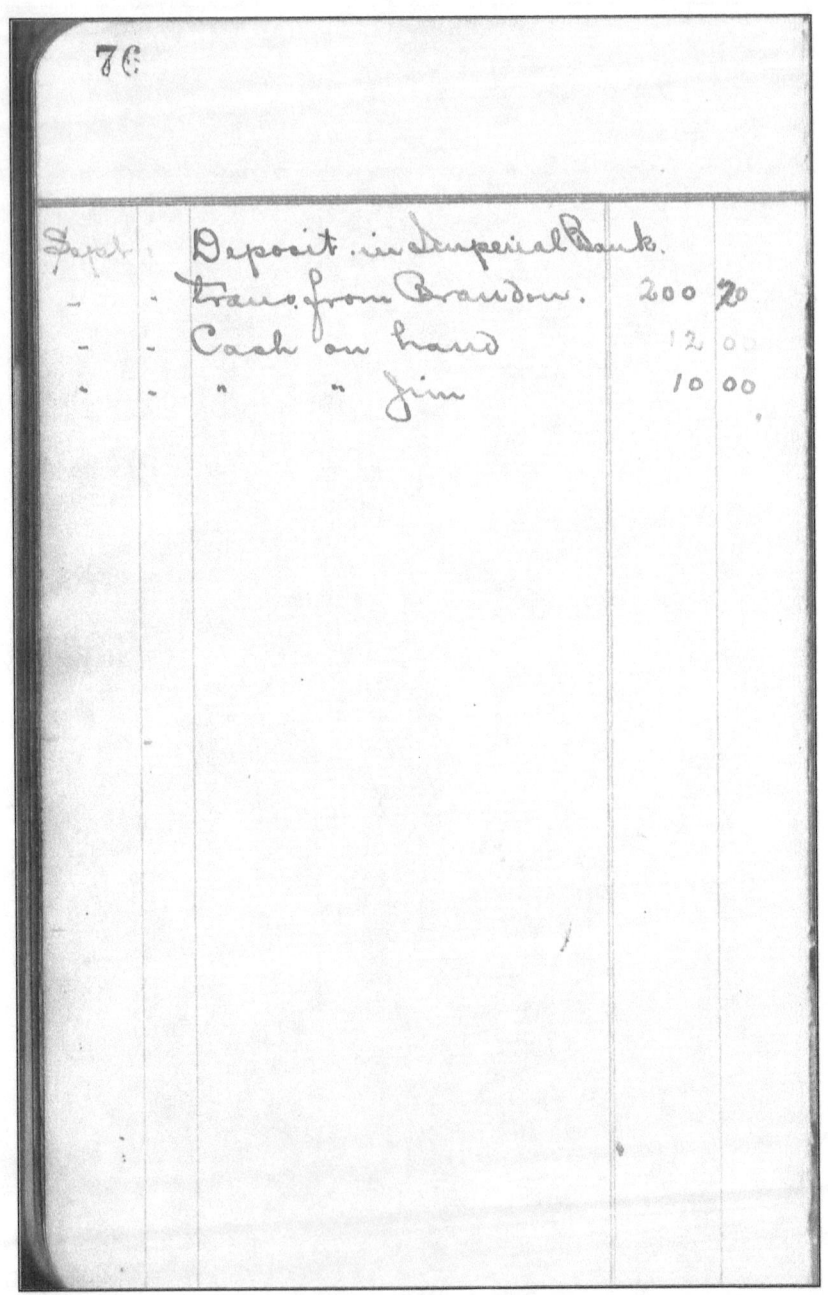

76

Sept	Deposit in Imperial Bank.		
	trans. from Brandon.	200	20
	Cash on hand	12	00
	" " Jim	10	00

PAGE 76 OF R.A. McRuer's cash journal.

77

Winnipeg. Sept ,st o6.

Aug	31	Fare to Winnipeg.	5	50
"	"	Transfer of Baggage. train		56
Sept	1	Expenses at Merchants hotel	1	50
"	"	Sundries		26
"	2	Exercise Books	1	50
"	"	Meal ticket	3	75
"	4	Stamps		10
"	"	Car Tickets		25
"	"	Writing Tablet		20
"	5	Suit of Clothes Semi Ready	25	00
"	"	Shoe polishes		25
"	"	" Polish		10
"	"	1 pair Slippers	2	50
"	"	1 pot Vaseline		10
"	"	1 Book + insist of the Wheat		50
"	"	Stamps		25
"	"	Waghorn Guide		10
"	8	Car Tickets		25
"	"	Ink		10
"	11	Foot-Ball		25
"	"	Scribbler		05
"	"	Free Press		05
			43	05

94				
	Winnipeg.			
Way	2	Balance.	39	85
"	5	Wages Braithwaite	5	00
			44	85
		On hand beginning major	234	10
		Check from Farmer	35	00
		Wages Braithwaite	20	00
			289	10

209
259
─────
$ 468.

PAGE 94 OF R.A. McRUER'S CASH JOURNAL.

Photos

95

May 1st, 1906

May	2	Car Fare Escan		25
-	5	Mrs McBride present	1	50
-	-	Banquet – Mariage	2	50
-	-	Meal Ticket	3	50
-	-	Sundries		60
-	7	Room for upr.	7	00
		Balance	29	50
			44	85
		Balance remaining at close May 7th	29	50
		Cost of Course	259	60
			289	10

PAGE 95 OF R.A. McRUER'S CASH JOURNAL.

217

MAIN STREET, BOISSEVAIN, MB. DATED 1908. NOTICE ELECTRICAL
POLES AND CONCRETE SIDEWALK. THESE ITEMS WERE NOT PART
OF THE SCENE WHEN ROBERT A. MCRUER LIVED IN TOWN.

218

FIVE MCRUER BROTHERS: JAMES, ROBERT, DANIEL, WILLIAM, AND JOHN.
DATE OF THE PHOTO IS UNKNOWN.

ROBERT A. McRUER'S DRUGSTORE, ST. BONIFACE, MB. 1906-1957.
DATE OF THE PHOTO IS UNKNOWN.

ROBERT A. McRUER IN HIS DRUGSTORE, ST. BONIFACE, MB.
DATE OF THE PHOTO IS UNKNOWN.

Bibliography for Allister of Turtle Mountain Series

Primary Sources:

Beckoning Hills History Book Committee (Ed.). *Beckoning Hills: Dawn of the New Millennium: Boissevain-Morton 1981–2006*. Brandon, MB: Leech Printing Ltd., 2006.

Boissevain History Committee (Ed.). *Beckoning Hills Revisited: Ours Is a Goodly Heritage: Morton-Boissevain, 1881–1981*. Altona, MB: Friesen Printers, 1981.

Musgrove, C. C., et al. (1956) *Beckoning Hills: Pioneer settlement Turtle Mountain Souris-Basin Areas*. Boissevain, Manitoba, Canada: 75th Jubilee Committee, 1956. (Map of pioneer settlement 1877-1881 in southwestern Manitoba. Map of pioneer settlement 1882-1886 in southwestern Manitoba).

Sears, Roebuck, and Co. Commemorative 1902 edition catalogue. Chicago, IL: Crown Publishers, 1969.

Secondary Sources:

_____, *Britannica Micropaedia* [Vol. 1] (15th ed.). s..v. "Ammonium Nitrate." Chicago: Britannica, 2002.

Artley, Bob. *Once upon a farm*. Gretna, LA: Pelican Publishing, 2000.

Bliss, Philip P. "Hallelujah, What a Savior!" 1875.

Bowers, Vivien. *Only in Canada: From the Colossal to the Kooky*. Toronto, ON: Maple Tree Press, Inc., 2002.

Bowers, Vivien. *Crazy about Canada!: Amazing Things Kids Want to Know*. Toronto, ON: Maple Tree Press, Inc., 2006.

Braun, Eric. *Canada in Pictures*. Minneapolis, MN: Lerner Publications, 2003.

Brooks, Phillips. "O Little Town of Bethlehem," 1865.

Bunyan, John. *Pilgrim's Progress*. Chicago: Moody Press, 1984. [First published in 1678].

Burns, Max. *Cottage Water Systems: An Out-of-the-City Guide to Pumps, Plumbing, Water Purification, and Privies*. Toronto, ON: Cottage Life Books, 1999.

_____, Calendars 1776–2000, Salt Lake City, Utah: Waters Clinic, Inc.

Cook, Ramsey. "Peopling the new Canada." Craig Brown (Ed.) *The Illustrated History of Canada*. Toronto, ON: Key Porter Books, 2002.

Crunican, Paul. *Priests and Politicians: Manitoba Schools and the Election of 1896*. Toronto, ON: University of Toronto Press, 1974.

Damerow, Gail. *Storey's Guide to Raising Chickens*. North Adam, MA: Storey Books, 1995.

Darnell, Regna. "Plains Cree." DeMollie, R. J., (Vol. Ed.) *Handbook of North American Indians* [Vol.13, Parts 1 & 2]. Washington: Smithsonian Institution, 2001.

Dickens, Charles. *A Christmas Carol and Other Stories*. New York, NY: Modern Library, 1995. [First published 1843].

Dickens, Charles. *David Copperfield*. New York, NY: Bantam Books, 1988. [First published 1868].

Dickens, Charles. *Great Expectations*. London, United Kingdom: Penguin Classics, 2009. [First published 1861].

Dix, William. "What Child is This?" 1865.

Durrell, Martin. "Word Order," in *Hammer's German Grammar and Usage* (3rd ed.). Lincolnwood, IL: NTC Publishing Group, 1997.

Flowerdew, Bob, and McVicar, Jekka. *Vegetables, Herbs and Fruit: An Illustrated Encyclopedia*. Richmond Hill, ON: Firefly Books, 2006.

Grove, Myrna J. *Legacy of One-Room Schools*. Morgantown, PA: Masthof Press, 2000.

Handy-Marchello, Barbara. *Women of the Northern Plains: Gender and Settlement on the Homestead Frontier 1870–1930*. St. Paul, MN: Minnesota Historical Society Press, 2005.

Hamilton, Janice. *Canada*. Minneapolis, MN: Carolrhoda Books, 1999.

_____, Interviews of former teachers and students of local rural schools Two archival videos, Fort Dauphin Museum, Dauphin, MB.

Jones, D. C., Sheehan, N. M., and Stamp, R. M. *Shaping the Schools of the Canadian West*. Calgary, Alberta: Detselig Enterprises, 1979.

Kalman, Bobbie. *Early Schools*. Niagara Falls, ON: Crabtree Publishing Co., 1991.

Lynch, Liz. "Inside the Parlor," in *Reminisce*. Glendale, WI: Reiman Media Group, Inc., 2007, April/May.

MacDonald, George. *At the Back of the North Wind*. New York, NY: Macmillan, 1964. [First published in 1871].

Mandelbaum, David. *The Plains Cree: An Ethnographic, Historical, and Comparative Study*. Regina, Saskatchewan: Canadian Plains Research Center, University of Regina, 1979.

Map of Manitoba. Markham, ON: Rand McNally Canada, Inc., 2007.

Melchior, Thomas. *They Called Me Teacher: Stories of Minnesota Country School Teachers and Students from 1915 to 1960*. Shakopee, MN: Melchior Publishing, 1997.

Middleton, Regina. "Hitting the Dusty Trail," in *Reminisce*. Glendale, WI: Reiman Media Group, Inc., 2006, October/November.

Munson, Edwin S. *World Book Encyclopedia* [Vol. 14]. s.v. "Nitrous Oxide." Chicago: World Book, Inc., 2009.

_____, *Britannica Micropaedia* [Vol. 8] (15th ed.). s.v. "Nitrous Oxide." Chicago: Britannica, 2002.

Palmer, T.H. "Try, Try Again," in *McGuffey's Fourth Eclectic Reader,* Revised Edition. New York, NY: American Book Co., 1920. [Originally published by Van Antwerp, Bragg & Co., 1879].

Pang, Guek-Cheng. *Canada*. Tarrytown, NY: Marshall Cavendish, 2004.

Patent, Dorothy Hinshaw. *Wheat, the Golden Harvest*. New York, NY: Dodd, Mead, 1987.

Peavy, Linda, and Smith, Ursula. *Frontier Children*. Norman, OK: University of Oklahoma Press, 1999.

Percy, Pam. *The Field Guide to Chickens*. St. Paul, MN: Voyageur Press, 2006.

Renier, Fernand G. "Description on Dutch Sounds," in *Beginner's Dutch*. New York: Hippocrene Books, Inc., 1999.

Salzmann, J. A. *Encyclopedia Americana* [Vol. 2], s.v. "History of Dentistry." Danbury, CT: Scholastic Library Publishing, 2005.

Staff. "Pictures from the Past." *Reminisce*. Glendale, WI: Reiman Media Group, Inc. 2007, February/March.

Stevenson, Robert Louis. *Treasure Island*. New York, NY: Simon and Schuster, Atheneum Books for Young Readers, 1911. [First published 1883].

Stevenson, Robert Louis. *Kidnapped*. New York, NY: Simon and Schuster, Atheneum Books for Young Readers, 2004. [First published 1886].

Sucher, Jaime J. *Shetland Sheepdogs*. Hauppauge, NY: Barron's Educational Services, Inc., 2000.

Vince, John. *Old Farms: An Illustrated Guide*. New York, NY: Schocken Books, 1982.

Wasilchick, John V. *Amish Life: A Portrait of Plain Living*. New York, NY: Crescent Books, 1991.

Wesley, Charles "Hark! The Herald Angels Sing," 1739.

Wordsworth, William. "My Heart Leaps up When I Behold." In *Major British Writers*. New York, NY: Harcourt, Brace, and World, Inc., 1959.

Wyss, Johann D. *Swiss Family Robinson*. New York, NY: Aladdin Paperbacks, 2007. [First published in 1812].

About the Author

Born in Winnipeg of Canadian parents, Patricia Linson spent her early years with her family in several states south of the border. Whenever she visited relatives in Winnipeg during her teen years, Robert A. McRuer, Patricia's grandfather, told stories of his life on a prairie homestead.

With the financial support of her grandfather, Patricia earned a degree in education. After becoming a naturalized citizen of the US, she began her teaching career as an elementary educator. Several years later, she went to graduate school for an MA in Teaching English to Speakers of Other Languages and for three years taught English as a Foreign Language in China. For a couple of decades thereafter, Patricia taught English as a Second Language to children and adults in several public schools in Minnesota.

After Patricia retired from teaching, she and her husband, Irv, travelled to southwestern Manitoba to see the McRuer farm for themselves before she wrote *Becoming Bob* and the Allister of Turtle Mountain Series.

Patricia lives with her husband, Irv, in Eagan, Minnesota, and keeps her horse, Grace, at a friend's rural stable. Irv and Patricia's daughter, son-in-law, and three of the four grandchildren live on a farm on the prairie of western Minnesota. The oldest grandson is attending university in St. Paul, Minnesota.

In *Book I: A Boy Called Allis,* eleven-year-old Allister McRuer's fears materialize the spring of 1892 when he and his family arrive at Cherry Creek, the town with the train depot closest to their Manitoba homestead claim. The first dread becomes a reality when Allister learns that the town's schoolhouse is too far from their farm for him and his twin brother, Jim, to walk to every day. How will Allister get any more schooling? While in Cherry Creek, Allister and Jim witness a terrible accident. Learning that the only doctor within seventy miles is out of town scares Allister. If someone in his family were to become sick or injured, who could he get to help? And what could make matters worse? Being called "Allis" constantly by his older brother, Will—who delights in taking advantage of Allister's quick temper.

In *Book II: Hope for Allis,* twelve-year-old Allister McRuer eagerly anticipates the opening of Wood Lake School, the one-room schoolhouse that he, his father, and brothers helped to build on a corner of his family's homestead. More than a year has passed, and Allister worries that he has forgotten everything he learned at his school in eastern Canada. Will he and his twin brother, Jim, ever be able to catch up? Allister's excitement quickly turns

to frustration. His new teacher can't seem to handle sixteen children in Grades 1 through 8. What chaos! And his father frustrates Allister further by constantly pulling him and Jim out of school to help with farm work or to build on their older brothers' homesteads. How are he and Jim going to pass any grade? Allister must also face the possibility of a schoolmate taunting him with the moniker "Allis," or worse. Should he take swings at the offender, like he did at his brother Will?

www.ingramcontent.com/pod-product-compliance
Lightning Source LLC
Chambersburg PA
CBHW051238250626
47155CB00009B/3079